The Ranch Was Not Going To Be The Same During Carly's Visit, And There Was No Pretending Otherwise.

But that was something he'd known before her arrival. What he hadn't anticipated or foreseen was the heart-pounding, throat-drying, gut-wrenching awareness in his own system caused by this woman. Not that he would do anything about it even if he wanted to, which, for his own peace of mind, he didn't. But she was his boss's daughter, for crying out loud, and even if he were the most dedicated of womanizers—as he'd once been—he would not touch his employer's daughter.

But oh, how he wanted to!

Dear Reader,

Silhouette is celebrating its 20th anniversary throughout 2000! So, to usher in the first summer of the millennium, why not indulge yourself with six powerful, passionate, provocative love stories from Silhouette Desire?

Jackie Merritt returns to Desire with a MAN OF THE MONTH who's *Tough To Tame*. Enjoy the sparks that fly between a rugged ranch manager and the feisty lady who turns his world upside down! Another wonderful romance from RITA Award winner Caroline Cross is in store for you this month with *The Rancher and the Nanny,* in which a rags-to-riches hero learns trust and love from the riches-to-rags woman who cares for his secret child.

Watch for Meagan McKinney's *The Cowboy Meets His Match*—an octogenarian matchmaker sets up an ice-princess heiress with a virile rodeo star. The Desire theme promotion THE BABY BANK, about sperm-bank client heroines who find love unexpectedly, concludes with Susan Crosby's *The Baby Gift*. Wonderful newcomer Sheri WhiteFeather offers another irresistible Native American hero with *Cheyenne Dad*. And Kate Little's hero reunites with his lost love in a marriage of convenience to save her from financial ruin in *The Determined Groom*.

So come join in the celebration and start your summer off on the supersensual side—by reading all six of these tantalizing Desire books!

Enjoy!

Joan Marlow Golan

Joan Marlow Golan
Senior Editor, Silhouette Desire

Please address questions and book requests to:
Silhouette Reader Service
U.S.: 3010 Walden Ave., P.O. Box 1325, Buffalo, NY 14269
Canadian: P.O. Box 609, Fort Erie, Ont. L2A 5X3

Tough To Tame
JACKIE MERRITT

Published by Silhouette Books
America's Publisher of Contemporary Romance

 SILHOUETTE BOOKS

ISBN 0-373-76297-6

TOUGH TO TAME

Visit Silhouette at www.eHarlequin.com

Printed in U.S.A.

JACKIE MERRITT

and her husband have settled once more in the Southwest after traveling around the West and Northwest for a while—Jackie wanted to soak up the atmosphere and find new locales and inspirations for her appealing Western stories.

IT'S OUR 20th ANNIVERSARY!
We'll be celebrating all year,
Continuing with these fabulous titles,
On sale in June 2000.

Romance

#1450 Cinderella's Midnight Kiss
Dixie Browning

#1451 Promoted–To Wife!
Raye Morgan

AN OLDER MAN

#1452 Professor and the Nanny
Phyllis Halldorson

The Circle K Sisters

#1453 Never Let You Go
Judy Christenberry

The WEDDING AUCTION

#1454 Contractually His
Myrna Mackenzie

#1455 Just the Husband She Chose
Karen Rose Smith

Desire

MAN OF THE MONTH

#1297 Tough To Tame
Jackie Merritt

#1298 The Rancher and the Nanny
Caroline Cross

MATCHED IN MONTANA

#1299 The Cowboy Meets His Match
Meagan McKinney

#1300 Cheyenne Dad
Sheri WhiteFeather

 #1301 The Baby Gift
Susan Crosby

#1302 The Determined Groom
Kate Little

Intimate Moments

 #1009 The Wildes of Wyoming–Ace
Ruth Langan

These Marrying McBrides! **#1010 The Best Man**
Linda Turner

#1011 Beautiful Stranger
Ruth Wind

#1012 Her Secret Guardian
Sally Tyler Hayes

#1013 Undercover with the Enemy
Christine Michels

#1014 The Lawman's Last Stand
Vickie Taylor

Special Edition

#1327 The Baby Quilt
Christine Flynn

 #1328 Irish Rebel
Nora Roberts

The Baby Set **#1329 To a MacAllister Born**
Joan Elliott Pickart

A Family Bond **#1330 A Man Apart**
Ginna Gray

DESERT ROGUES **#1331 The Sheik's Secret Bride**
Susan Mallery

#1332 The Price of Honor
Janis Reams Hudson

One

The long-distance telephone conversation began as usual; Stuart "Stu" Paxton, calling from his home in New York, asked how things were going at his ranch in Wyoming. What was unusual was the reply of the ranch manager, Jake Banyon. "I'm afraid we have a problem, Stu. A strange stallion has been gathering himself a harem of our mares. He collected one the other night and two more just last night."

"A *strange* stallion, Jake? I'm not following."

"Neither am I," Jake said grimly. "Truth is I have no idea where he came from or who he belongs to. If he belongs to anyone, that is. He appears to be completely on his own."

"Surely you're not thinking he's a wild horse," Stuart said, sounding skeptical.

"It's not impossible, Stu, though to be perfectly honest he has the conformation lines of good breeding. Course, I've only seen him once and that was from a distance."

"And he just showed up? A full-grown stallion? Jake, he had to come from somewhere. With the ranch being so isolated and all, I mean, he didn't just trot over from a neighbor's field.''

''Exactly. I've put an ad in the *Tamarack* newspaper describing him. If anyone in this county owns him, they'll be calling. In the meantime, I've got men out every day trying to locate his lair. I'd like to get those mares back.''

''And if you manage to capture him?''

''That's hard to say without getting a closer look at him.'' Jake was intimating that if the stallion did belong to someone, the horse might be carrying tattoos or brands identifying his owner.

Stu grasped the concept at once. ''Makes sense. Well, let me know what happens.''

''Will do.'' Jake then started talking about other events on the 4,000-acre Wild Horse Ranch, owned by the Paxton family for almost a century. Stuart hadn't taken to the isolation and business of raising cattle, as his ancestors had, and he'd left the ranch right out of high school and, to this day, only went back two or three times a year. Since his father's death ten years before, Stuart had relied entirely on hired help to keep the place going. Even though he didn't want to live in Wyoming, he couldn't bring himself to sell his birthright. He'd run into some bad apples posing as ranch managers, however, and now claimed to be extremely fortunate to have a man of Jake Banyon's knowledge and expertise at the helm. During their four-year working relationship, the two men— even though Stuart was twenty years older than Jake—had formed a durable bond of mutual respect.

Jake was still talking about current affairs at the ranch when Stuart interrupted. ''Jake, sorry to break in like this, but I called tonight for a reason. I need a favor. Uh, it's a personal favor.''

Stuart sounded anxious, which startled Jake. If ever he'd met a more confident, self-assured man than Stuart Paxton, he couldn't remember it. Nor, he realized, could he recall Stuart ever asking for, or even mentioning, a ''personal favor." This was a first, and it made Jake sit up and take notice. He would, after all, do just about anything for Stuart.

Jake had grown up on a ranch—same as Stuart—but that was the only similarity between the two men's early years. Stuart went to college and then proceeded to make a name and a fortune for himself in the business world. Jake's home had been in Montana. He had finished high school but he'd been too far gone on a local girl to consider leaving her to attend college—a disappointment for his father. But he'd worked as a cowhand for his dad and made plans with Gloria to get married in August.

When August rolled around that summer, however, Gloria gave him back his ring and announced that she'd met someone else. "Sorry," she'd said calmly.

Jake went a little crazy. He was nineteen years old and believed his life was over. Everyone had advice for him, none of it meant a damn. He loved a girl who'd met "someone else," and there was nothing he could do about it. He had never felt so helpless in his life, especially when Gloria moved away and no one would tell him where she'd gone.

He started going from woman to woman—the wilder the better—until his father gruffly told him to wake up and smell the coffee. "Jake, you're drinking too much, and I can't depend on you anymore. Find yourself another job."

Years passed. Jake's downward slide went from bad to worse, and he'd pretty much hit rock bottom when he'd finally gotten a whiff of that coffee his dad had talked about. It was at his father's funeral—his mother had died long before—when something inside of him seemed to cave in and he saw a painfully clear image of what he'd been doing to himself over a girl who probably never had loved him. He vowed on the spot to be the kind of man his dad had been— hardworking and clean-living. He would, of course, run the family ranch.

Only there no longer was a family ranch. The bank foreclosed, and Jake—totally stunned and shaken—had tried to make some sense out of the shambles of his life. His old friends—especially the women—couldn't understand why he avoided them or why he wasn't hanging out at his favorite watering holes.

To make a complete break with the past, Jake left Montana and went to Wyoming to find work, and he just happened to stop in a little town called Tamarack. While eating supper in a café he read the local newspaper and saw an ad for a ranch manager. That was how he met Stuart Paxton, and to this day Jake still considered it a miracle that Stuart had taken a chance on the transient, down-on-his-luck stumblebum he'd been four years ago.

Jake's most profound regret was that his parents, especially his father, had not lived to see the man he was today. He worked hard, he was physically strong and fit, he didn't smoke, drink or chase wild women. In fact, the pendulum had swung so far in the other direction that Jake had become an antisocial loner. That was one reason he loved the Wild Horse Ranch; it was eighty miles from Tamarack, the nearest town, and he didn't have to even set eyes on a woman unless he wanted to take that long drive, which didn't happen often. His sex drive, once so outrageously out of control, was now banked and mostly forgotten. Jake questioned his wasted youth and wished he had it to do over again. He should have gone to college when Gloria broke their engagement. He should have behaved like a man, taken her rejection on the chin and gotten on with life instead of floundering in self-pity for so many years. All he could do, he'd finally decided, was to accept the way he had once lived and be proud of the way he lived now, sincerely believing that he had Stuart Paxton to thank for everything he'd accomplished.

It was the reason he said quietly, "Stu, whatever you need, if I can help out, all you have to do is name it."

"Thanks, Jake. I knew I could count on you. Okay, here's the situation. You've heard me mention my daughter Carly."

"Uh, sure, Stu. What about her?" Actually, Jake just

barely recalled Stu talking about his daughter, probably because Jake simply hadn't been interested enough to retain the memory. Stuart's wife had died many years ago, and Jake did remember—vaguely—Stuart saying something about the difficulties of raising a daughter without her mother.

"I brought Carly to the ranch a couple of times when she was a little girl, but then in her teens she decided she didn't like it, so I didn't force her to go with me when I went to Wyoming. She hasn't been there for about fifteen years. Anyhow, this past year has really been tough on her—her divorce, you know—and, Jake, it breaks my heart to see her so unhappy. She's trying so damned hard to pick up the pieces and start a new life that she deserves a medal. But I think she still can't believe that a man could be as...as phony and despicable as her ex was."

Jake frowned. There was something Stuart wasn't saying, Jake could hear the hesitation, the holdback, in Stuart's voice. But Jake really didn't want to hear any sordid details about anyone's divorce—anyone else's personal problems, for that matter, because he had more harsh memories of his own than any one person deserved—so he didn't encourage Stuart to say more than he had. Instead, he murmured quietly, "What is it you want me to do?" He heard his employer draw a long breath before he spoke.

"I've been thinking that a change of scene just might give Carly a whole new perspective. Jake, would you mind if I sent her to the ranch for a visit?"

Jake's whole body stiffened with instantaneous dread. It was all he could do to say something even remotely sensible. "It's your ranch," he mumbled.

"But you're running it, Jake. It's your home, and if Carly's presence would bother you in any way..."

Jake had gotten his wits together—some of them, at least. "No, no, Stu," he said, abruptly cutting in. "Carly is more than welcome here. Anytime."

"You're sure?"

"Positive." Jake's mouth was so dry he felt parched. The ranch was a strictly male society. Even the cook was a man. The house was old, rundown and not especially clean. Jake was the only person who used the house at all; every other man on the place slept in the bunkhouse.

But Stuart knew all that, Jake thought uneasily. When Stuart came to the ranch, he used one of the four bedrooms on the second floor. There were boots and clothes in that particular room's closet and bureau, things that Stuart deliberately left behind so he wouldn't be hauling them back and forth between New York and Wyoming.

There were no bedrooms on the first floor, which meant that Carly would be sleeping upstairs, same as Jake. It flashed through Jake's mind that he could move into the bunkhouse during her visit, but he hated giving up his privacy so much that he immediately retreated from that idea. He *needed* his privacy, he could not live with a bunch of men. And the crew wouldn't like it, either. Jake had never attempted to be buddies with his men, and if he moved into the bunkhouse now, everyone on the place would be uncomfortable.

"I think Carly remembers some things about the ranch," Stuart said. "When I brought her there as a child, my folks were still living, of course, so her memories could be more about her grandparents than about the ranch itself. But it's a nice quiet place, Jake—which I think she needs right now— and she will own it someday, so there's more than one reason why she should spend some time in Wyoming."

"Anything you say, Stu." Jake marveled at the normalcy of his voice when his pulse was leaping around erratically and his palms were sweaty. Everything had been just about perfect for four years now, ever since he'd set foot on Wild Horse Ranch. A woman on the place—any woman—would change the very air they all breathed. The men smoked, chewed tobacco, spit and cussed wherever and whenever they felt like it. They told off-color jokes and made crude references to females in general, even though most of them were married or had girlfriends and would defend the reputations of their own women to the death, if challenged.

But that was all stuff that Stuart knew, too, Jake thought. Stuart had grown up among cowhands, and there was one thing they both knew they could rely on. Cowboys might be tough talkers and hard as nails with other men, but they were respectful and often shy around a lady. Now, if the lady turned out to be not so ladylike, that was a different story, but the truth was that most cowhands—just like most men in any line of work—took their cue from the woman.

Actually, Jake admitted with a knot of anxiety in his gut, it wasn't the men he was worried about if Carly really did come to the ranch; it was himself. He liked the status quo. He liked eating in the cookshack with the crew and not having to worry about meals. How would Carly take eating with a bunch of strange men?

Of course, there again Stuart knew the score, and Jake didn't think it was his place to suggest that his employer's daughter might not enjoy some of the routines on the ranch.

"When, uh, do you think she'll be coming?"

"Probably in a week or so. I'll let you know for sure."

"Do you want me to meet her plane in Cheyenne?"

"No, I think I'll hire a helicopter for the trip from Cheyenne to the ranch. I'll let you know when everything comes together," Stuart said.

"Yeah, okay," Jake mumbled. They talked a few more minutes, but when Jake hung up he couldn't remember what they'd said. He really felt as though the life he had created for himself on this beautiful piece of Wyoming land was slipping away. A rational part of his brain told him not to panic or jump to conclusions. After all, Carly Paxton might be a perfectly nice person who would fit in so smoothly that no one on the ranch would even be aware of her presence.

"Yeah, right," Jake muttered with a dark scowl on his face. Getting up from the desk he'd been sitting at in the room used as an office in the house, he headed for the front door and stepped outside onto the wide, wraparound porch. This was a favorite after-dark retreat. The crew was somewhere in the vicinity of the bunkhouse—smoking, talking and just hanging around until bedtime—but that building was behind the main house, along with the barns and corrals, the sheds and such. Jake always felt pretty much alone on the front porch, and when the weather was good—as it was now, in late June—he spent a lot of evenings out there. It was a good place to think and to formulate the men's work schedules. The seasons pretty much determined the cycle of work on cattle ranches, but there were still decisions to be made about which man should be doing what.

Settling himself into a chair, Jake inhaled deeply and attempted to reason away the knot of anxiety in his gut. That exercise raised a question: Who was he now? He was not the same man he'd been after Gloria dumped him, nor was he like the other cowhands on the ranch. He couldn't compare himself to Stuart, who possessed almost a magical talent for making money and who certainly lived in a much bigger world than Jake did.

The word *misfit* entered Jake's mind, and he sighed heavily. He couldn't deny being a misfit, nor could he deny the bitterness he still felt toward all women because of what one had done to him, even though he kept it fairly well under control. For instance, it was not a subject he had ever discussed with Stuart. In fact, he hadn't talked about his past with anyone since coming to Wyoming. Wasn't it rather peculiar that he couldn't get rid of the bitterness when he'd stopped seeing Gloria so long ago?

Jake thinned his lips. He hated these moments when he tried to analyze himself. Good Lord, he was no worse than any other man on the place. Everyone had problems and not everyone had solutions. He would live through Carly's visit and, in the meantime, he'd do a little praying that she still wouldn't like the ranch and her stay would be brief.

Other than worry, what else *could* he do?

* * *

This helicopter ride is by far the best part of today's trip, Carly thought while gaping at the Wyoming landscape below the aircraft. She had very little memory of the openness, the lack of population, and realized that the things she did remember from childhood visits to the Paxton ranch were from a child's point of view and possibly contradictory to the reality of this remote part of the world.

Today she was fascinated with the occasional huddles of buildings she saw—obviously other ranches, for the most part few and far between—and the almost traffic-free roads, the immense fields and pastures dwarfing herds of cattle and antelope. The beauty of the distant mountains—the Tetons— actually took her breath, and she felt something sigh within her, a whisper of serenity she hadn't felt in a very long time.

Carly really hadn't wanted to come to Wyoming, and had agreed to her father's suggestion merely to alleviate his concern for her. She had caused him terrible worries in the past year and had decided that a trip to Wyoming was a very small sacrifice for her to make, if it made her dad feel better.

Now, seeing the area for herself, through adult eyes, she realized there was no sacrifice involved. Who would not appreciate the vastness of uncluttered valleys and the grandeur of distant mountains, such as she was viewing? Small wonder that her father had become excited whenever he'd planned a trip to the ranch.

The pilot touched her arm to get her attention. "Your destination is just ahead," he told her. "We'll be landing in that field to the right of the house." The copter began descending.

Carly found the spot the pilot had indicated and the corners of her lips tipped into a little half smile when she found herself nostalgically remembering the large two-story house, with its wraparound porch, and the numerous old shade trees in the yard. Attempting to absorb everything at once, her gaze moved to the barns, sheds and corrals. The lower the copter dropped, the more details she could see.

Then, movement farther out caught her eye, and she spotted two men on horseback, riding hard it seemed, trailing some distance behind a third horse. Were the men trying to catch the riderless horse? For some reason, Carly wanted to know what was happening.

"Could you get closer to those three horses?" she asked the pilot.

"Sure, no problem," he told her.

The helicopter swung to the right and dropped lower, until it was just above the treetops. Carly could see the two riders look up and knew that the copter had startled them. At almost the same moment she got an unobstructed view of the third horse, the one without a rider.

"Oh, he's magnificent," she whispered in awe. The horse was black as coal, and his hide glistened with perspiration in the waning afternoon light. Why on earth were those two men running him so hard? Had he escaped a stall or corral? "What do you think is going on?" she asked the pilot.

"Looks like the men on horseback are trying to rope the third horse. They're both carrying ropes."

"Oh, yes, I see that now." The black horse suddenly disappeared in a heavy stand of timber, and a minute later so did the two men and their mounts. Carly felt a pang of disappointment. She would have liked very much to see the outcome of that chase.

"Okay if we land now?" the pilot asked.

"Yes, of course. Thanks for the detour."

"No problem at all. As I told you when we met, I've flown your father out to the ranch many times. He sometimes requests a few detours along the way."

Carly smiled. "Like father, like daughter?" Carly liked being favorably compared to her father, even though she knew their personalities differed in some very crucial ways. Stuart was a laid-back easygoing guy, which sometimes gave people an erroneous impression of his intelligence and perspicacity, particularly in business. Carly, on the other hand, was high-strung, excitable and quick to speak her mind. Plus, even with a high IQ, she had inherited very little of her father's talent for spotting a money-making deal and then knowing exactly what to do about it.

There was one more trait Carly wished she had inherited from her dad: He was an incredibly good judge of character, and she fell really short in that department. Her awful marriage was proof of that, and she wondered now if she would ever trust her own judgment of a man again. Not that she was in any kind of rush for another personal, so-called romantic relationship. Her entire system shied from the idea whenever it passed through her mind, and she didn't doubt that it could be a very long time before she let herself be caught in that trap again. In truth, she had come to believe that the whole concept of romance was nothing more than media hype to sell magazines and expensive products to lily-livered women who believed they simply could not live any sort of productive life without a man. She was no longer in that category, thank God. Instead of the romantic little fool she'd once been, she was now a down-to-earth, unromantic, unsentimental, no-nonsense realist. No sweet-talking, butter-wouldn't-melt-in-his-mouth man was ever going to pull the wool over her eyes again. She believed it with every fiber of her being.

The pilot, a pleasant, older man, smiled back. "No crime in that."

Carly smiled again, but said no more. They were about to land and she could see a tall lanky man in jeans, boots and a big hat standing at the edge of the field.

When Jake heard the approaching helicopter, he had immediately headed for the landing field. He'd stood there frowning when the copter veered off in another direction. But he'd been able to follow its course well enough and had watched until it turned around.

Jake was admittedly nervous about this first meeting with Stuart's daughter. To be perfectly honest, he'd *been* nervous

since he'd lied to Stuart on the phone and said that Carly
was welcome to visit the ranch anytime. She wasn't welcome, no woman was, and Jake had been wishing for everything from a pilot's strike canceling flights to Wyoming to a
flu virus hitting the entire country that wouldn't kill anyone
but would sure keep them from traveling. Those were silly
wishes, of course. Nothing was going to prevent Carly's visit,
and that fact had sank in a little deeper every day until now
it seemed to gnaw at the very center of Jake's bones.

It was especially unnerving that instead of landing immediately, the copter had flown a circle over the ranch compound. Since the pilot would have no reason to make that
aerial tour, then Carly must have asked him to do it.

*Hell, why wouldn't she want to get a good look at the
ranch? She hasn't been here since she was a kid.*

That argument, though sensible, didn't elevate Jake's dark
mood by much. If Carly was the kind of woman to throw
her weight around because her dad owned the ranch, then
there wasn't a snowball's chance in hell of the two of them
getting along. And if they didn't get along, wouldn't it affect
his and Stuart's relationship?

Jake's lips thinned from an abrupt onslaught of tension.
He couldn't let anything destroy, or even maim, his and Stuart's working relationship. He and Carly Paxton—Stuart had
told him that she'd resumed her maiden name after the divorce—*had* to get along, even if it meant his kowtowing to
an overbearing woman's whims. Mumbling a curse over that
image, Jake watched the copter descend and finally settle on
the ground.

The pilot cut the engine, and Jake began walking toward
the aircraft. He had a terrible knot in his gut and something
else almost as uncomfortable—a premonition. From this moment on his life was not going to be the same.

"Damn," he muttered under his breath. "Dammit to
hell."

Two

Carly unhooked her seat belt with her gaze on the tall man coming forth. He had to be Jake Banyon, but he wasn't at all what she'd expected. How had she gotten the impression that the ranch's manager was much older? She was approaching thirty, and Banyon looked to be about the same. On top of that surprise was another: he was good-looking! Taking in his long, lean body clad in snug, faded jeans and a blue work shirt, and the ruggedly handsome—though hard—features of his face, Carly felt an unmistakably sexual flutter in the pit of her stomach.

The sensation startled then angered her, and she set her lips into a thin, grim line. This visit just might be cut very short, she thought resentfully, although she had packed for a long stay just in case she happened to like the ranch. *Dad could have told me Banyon was young and good-looking. Why didn't he ever mention it?*

The pilot hopped out of his side of the copter, called a hello to Jake and then opened the door for Carly. She put her feet on the ground just as Jake walked up, took off his hat with one hand and offered the other.

"Jake Banyon," he said tonelessly and without a smile. "Welcome to Wild Horse Ranch."

"Thank you," Carly said stiffly, giving his hand a quick shake and then pulling hers back as though she had just touched something poisonous. Actually, the warmth and life of his working man's calloused hand had sent shock waves through her system that nearly caused her to panic right in Banyon's face.

Good Lord, she thought in the next uneasy breath, except for the sniffing and smelling we are sizing each other up like two strange dogs!

It was true. Jake was shaken because Carly was tall and slender, with stunning green eyes and long dark hair. He'd hoped—ardently—that she would be ordinary, 'very ordinary', and she wasn't. She was appealingly female and would stand out in any crowd.

Carly's thoughts were similar and horribly perturbing. Banyon had the bluest eyes she'd ever seen, a head of almost black hair and darkly tanned skin. There was no warmth in those incredible eyes, but even cold and guarded they were drop-dead gorgeous. She'd been so positive that she would not be affected by a man for a long, long time and here she was feeling feverish and giddy around a damn cowboy. It was totally unacceptable, and any remnants of panic she'd felt a minute ago vanished and were replaced by a defiant determination to remain on her family's ranch for as long as she wanted. No way was she going to let a good-looking cowboy scare her off.

The pilot was taking luggage from the cargo compartment and setting the suitcases on the ground. It was a nice, safe subject, and Jake used it to get himself thinking about something other than Carly's long legs and impressive figure, displayed nicely but provocatively—he thought—in a pair of fitted jeans and a blue-and-red striped shirt.

"I'm going to move your luggage away from the copter," he said. "Then I'll walk you up to the house. I'll have a couple of the men bring in your suitcases."

Carly almost said, "Walking me to the house won't be necessary. I'm sure I can find it on my own." But she stopped herself in time and murmured instead, "That will be fine." As Jake walked over to the pilot and luggage, Carly whispered, "That nicety was for you, Dad." It wasn't Banyon's fault that his good looks and age unnerved her, and neither could she condemn her father for not better describing Banyon during conversations about the ranch and Wyoming. *Dad probably hasn't even noticed that Jake is good-looking, and why would he?*

Truth was, she thought uneasily, she could tell that she was as much of a surprise for Jake as he was for her. This was not a comfortable situation for either of them. She knew about the bunkhouse and that Jake was the only person occupying the house. She knew about the cookhouse and that the men took their meals in an attached dining room. Her father had—at least—emphasized those points again, in case she'd forgotten past discussions, and he'd told her that she could eat with the men or prepare her own meals in the house, whichever she preferred. His final advice had been to "relax and enjoy yourself, honey."

Carly turned to scan the peaceful green fields that stretched for miles in every direction, then the foothills to the west and finally the mountainous horizon. One would have to look long and hard for a more perfect place in which to relax, but something told her that she would have found relaxation much easier to attain if Banyon had been twenty years older, bald and bowlegged.

She lowered her eyebrows, frowning over her own narrowed eyes as she contemplated her unexpected and extremely unwelcome physical reactions to Jake Banyon. She was positive she would be as irate over an attraction to any man at this stage of her life. She needed more time to heal, for God's sake. The emotional wounds from her frightening farce of a marriage were barely scarred over, and in all honesty the mere thought of romance made her shudder. Romance was merely an illusion, anyhow, she now believed, a short-term ploy that men used to get women right where they wanted them. Once that was accomplished and men started showing their true colors, their women had better watch out.

Heaving a sigh, Carly pushed those dreadful thoughts from her mind and looked at Banyon and the pilot moving her luggage a safe distance from the helicopter. She decided then and there that however magnetic she found Banyon to be, he was never going to know about it, primarily because she was not going to let a meaningless physical attraction override her common sense. She wasn't ready for anything but the most distant of friendships with any member of the opposite sex, and until she was ready, this and any other relationship with a man would be chilly indeed.

The two men shook hands, the pilot called a goodbye to her and returned to the cabin of his aircraft. Carly moved away from the copter and stood near her suitcases.

Jake walked up. "Your things will be fine here for a few minutes. Let's go up to the house now."

"All right." She spoke without really looking at him, and she began walking when he did. The helicopter took off, and the turbulence caused by the rotors tossed her hair around. Smoothing it down, she chanced a quick glance at Banyon. "I hope this visit is not too much of an intrusion," she said coolly.

"Don't worry about it."

"Sounds like you are," she said bluntly.

"I'm what?"

"Worried. Well, don't be. I promise to stay out of your hair."

Can you? Are you capable of entertaining yourself and staying out of everyone's way? Jake doubted it. The ranch

was not going to be the same during Carly's visit, and there
was no pretending otherwise.

But that was something he'd known before her arrival.
What he hadn't anticipated or foreseen was the heart-
pounding, throat-drying, gut-wrenching awareness in his own
system caused by this woman. Not that he would do anything
about it even if he wanted to, which he didn't, for his own
peace of mind. But she was Stuart's daughter, for crying out
loud. And even if he were the most dedicated of womanizers—as he'd once been—he would not touch his employer's
daughter. It was more than that, though; he respected Stuart
far too much to risk offending him by making a pass at his
daughter.

All of those surprising feelings and thoughts aside, however, Jake felt an obligation to make Stuart's daughter feel
welcome. "You're not an intrusion, and I'm not worried
about anything. In fact, I sincerely hope you enjoy your
stay."

She didn't believe a word of it. Tone of voice was so much
more telling than words, and he really sounded as though
he'd just eaten some sour grapes. The truth came to her in a
flash. Banyon had agreed to her visiting the ranch because
her father had put it to him in a way he hadn't been able to
gracefully refuse.

Carly was thinking of the bond between her dad and Jake
Banyon when he asked, "How was your trip?"

In Carly's opinion that was one of those questions people
asked when they didn't know what else to say. But it indicated that he was trying to make the best of things, and could
she do any less?

"Long," she said a bit dryly, then remembered that it
hadn't all been boring. "The helicopter ride was enjoyable,
and let me ask you about something I saw from the air when
we were approaching the ranch. Two men on horseback were
chasing a third horse. Or they appeared to be chasing it. Do
you know what was going on?"

Jake abruptly stopped walking to stare at her. "Was the third horse black?"

What a peculiar reaction to a simple question, Carly thought. She certainly had gotten his full attention with it. Standing her ground, she stared back, though he really didn't seem to notice. Apparently he was still intent on the third horse, which seemed odd to Carly.

Still, he was obviously anxious about her reply, so she didn't keep him waiting. "The third horse was black as pitch, and probably one of the most beautiful horses I've ever seen," she recited, wondering if that was the information he was seeking.

"That damned devil stallion!" Jake's eyes bore an angry light. "He's getting bolder. I sure hope those men you saw captured him."

"What?" Carly's confusion showed on her face. "Did he escape…or something?"

"Escape! He doesn't belong to this ranch. He doesn't belong to anybody, as far as I can tell. He's wild as a March wind, and he's stealing our mares."

Carly frowned. "I don't get it. I mean, are wild horses common around here?"

"They used to be," Jake said grimly. "The story is that about a hundred years ago a cavalry unit turned a bunch of horses loose in this part of Wyoming. The herd multiplied for a while, then began dying out. I haven't heard of anyone spotting any of those mustangs in years. Then, out of the blue, that black stallion showed up and started gathering himself a harem of our best mares."

Jake started walking again, and Carly hurried to keep stride. "I still don't understand," she said. "I've read about wild horses and seen pictures of them, and that stallion doesn't look at all like the mustangs in those photos."

"I know he doesn't. He looks like he comes from good stock, but I've tried everything I know to locate his owner, with no luck. The only conclusion I've been able to come up with is that a mustang mated with a mare of good lineage and the result was that stallion.''

"I guess that theory makes sense," Carly murmured, intrigued by the "mystery" stallion and where he'd come from. "And he's been collecting a harem, as you put it?''

"He's already managed to lure away five of our mares."

"Is he luring mares from other ranches, as well?''

"Not that I've heard."

He'd spoken so curtly, so brusquely, that Carly sent him a quick, curious glance. Banyon struck her as one of those people who would rather stew silently than talk about a problem. And while he'd already had the wild stallion problem to deal with before today, her arrival had obviously given him another one. She sensed that he would rather not talk about the stallion, but she really didn't care what he preferred. Her curiosity had been piqued and she wanted to know everything he did.

"Would you say that he considers this ranch his home territory?'' she asked.

"God only knows," Jake muttered.

"Well, this is a huge ranch. Maybe he was born here."

"It's possible."

Carly was positive that he'd grunted those two words. Obviously the topic unnerved Banyon, and so did her insistence on talking about it. But they had clashed at first sight, she told herself, so why worry now about soothing the savage beast, so to speak? Banyon seemed to be as untamed as this country, a raw, ill-bred, boringly macho guy whose favorite pastimes probably included tractor pulls and those perfectly awful arena shows where men driving old clunker cars deliberately ran into each other.

Besides, she really didn't care if Banyon liked her or not, though it was not something she'd thought about before meeting him, and if she wanted to say something, she'd do it.

"Well," she drawled, "I guess this ranch is appropriately named."

Jake sent her a look of utter disgust. "Losing good mares to a rogue stallion is not funny."

"No, but it is interesting. Wild Horse Ranch is being stormed by a wild stallion. Yes, I find that quite interesting. Tell me, if and when you capture him, what will you do with him?"

"Some of the men think we should shoot him."

Carly's eyes got huge from shock. "You wouldn't! Does Dad know about this?"

"He knows." They had finally reached the lawn around the house. Jake had had enough conversation about that stallion and, in fact, was anxious to deposit Carly in the house so he could go and find the men who had been chasing that devil. It would be an incredible stroke of luck if they'd caught him.

Carly still wasn't through with the subject, however. "I can't believe Dad would agree to killing such a beautiful animal, just because he's a nuisance," she said with distinct disapproval.

Jake stopped walking and faced her. He spoke gruffly, impatiently. "Let me set the record straight. First of all, I said some of the *men* think we should shoot that horse. I didn't say how I felt about it. Second, that stallion is not just a nuisance. He's a damn thief, and as long as he's running wild he's going to keep on increasing his herd of mares. Do you think a rancher should ignore the loss of valuable horses? Your father doesn't think so, and neither do I." Spinning on his heel, Jake headed for the house.

Carly ran to catch up. "So you're not going to shoot him?"

"I didn't say that, either," Jake growled, surprising himself with a comment that indicated he might decide to shoot the stallion, when, in fact, he'd never once considered that option. He was not an animal killer, never had been. He didn't even like hunting. But that stallion had him on edge, Carly herself had him on edge, and he wished to high heaven that she would just stop talking about it.

She knew what he wished, which was kind of strange as reading other people's minds was not a common occurrence for her. But Banyon's annoyance was so obvious. He actually looked pained, as though she or some unseen thing was sticking pins into him.

Well, that was just tough. No one was going to shoot that horse while she was here, and Banyon might as well know from the get-go how she felt about it. Besides, she didn't particularly like the tone of voice he was using with her, as though no one but him even had a right to an opinion about that stallion.

"Maybe I should also set the record straight," she said coolly. "I didn't come here with any intentions of questioning your authority on any aspect of the operation of this ranch. You and Dad apparently have a mutually acceptable working agreement, which I fully intended to honor. But I will not sit by calmly and permit you or anyone else to shoot a horse that is only doing what his nature demands."

They had reached the stairs to the front porch. Jake stopped in his tracks and turned to her with his eyes narrowed, thinking, so she is the kind of woman to throw her weight around! And, as galling as it was, she had a right. Or she would have someday, when she inherited the ranch.

In the meantime, he took his orders from her dad—on the rare occasion when Stuart Paxton issued an order—and Carly might as well understand right now that he would not put up with interference from her or anyone other than Stuart about how he ran the ranch.

"Exactly what would you do about it if we did shoot that stallion?" Jake asked in a chilling, challenging voice.

Carly hadn't expected to be so openly challenged, and her heart sank a little. But then she lifted her chin. A confrontation with Banyon within fifteen minutes of her arrival was startling, but if she didn't stand her ground now she would look spineless and without convictions and standards strong enough to fight for. It was the way she'd behaved during her marriage, and she had vowed to never again permit a man to ride roughshod over feelings she had every right to possess.

But her next thought—Jake Banyon was nothing like her ex. Banyon, in fact, might not be like anyone she'd ever known—made her wonder if open warfare with him was wise.

Still, should she cower and withdraw from a serious issue just because Banyon had an overwhelming personality?

She stood her ground and said in a voice every bit as challenging as Jake's, ''I'm sure there are laws against killing animals you don't own.''

''There are also laws permitting ranchers to protect the animals they do own from predators,'' Jake snapped. The anger in his system alarmed him, and he had to ask himself what was causing it, the topic under debate or Carly's pretty face and blatant sexuality. He didn't deserve this, dammit, he didn't. He'd sown his wild oats years ago and he didn't need any reminders that he'd been living without sex for a long time. Living contentedly, for a fact. Now, this very minute, his body was stirring in ways he'd practically forgotten and sure hadn't missed.

Jake told himself to calm down, to tell Carly that he never had planned to kill that stallion, which would stop this ridiculous controversy here and now. But when he opened his mouth to enlighten her, he heard himself saying instead, speaking harshly, ''I've got work to do. Let's go inside and get this over with.''

Carly almost gasped out loud. Banyon's rudeness was insulting and infuriating, and she took a deep breath to thwart the torrent of angry words she would have loved to lay on him. But while she managed to control the worst of her ire, she couldn't stop herself from giving him a venomous look, or from saying, ''Believe me, I do not need your assistance to walk into this house. It's been a while since I've been here, but I'm not the complete moron you seem to think I am.'' Brushing past him, she climbed the stairs and crossed the porch to the front door.

Jake stared after her. She certainly had a temper, he thought, while he tried to control his own. It was when he was striding away from the house that regret hit him hard and suddenly. That had been a stupid way to start Carly's visit, especially when he had vowed to get along with her. What he probably should do was to return to the house, locate Carly and apologize.

But maybe she was the one who should do the apologizing, he decided in the next heartbeat, stubbornly continuing his walk to the barns while hoping those two men had captured that stallion. Dammit, he'd known a woman on the place would disrupt its peace—*his* peace—and he'd sure been right about that.

In this instance, though, being right didn't make him feel better, and he wore a sour expression all the way to the barns.

Inside the house Carly came very close to completely forgetting that Jake Banyon even existed. It was the house from her childhood memories, but it was so sadly run-down that it broke her heart. Going from room to room on the first floor, she nostalgically touched things—the rocking chair near the living room fireplace that her grandfather had favored, and the old upright piano against a wall on which her grandmother had played merry tunes.

Carly's troubled gaze swept the old wallpaper and worn furnishings. How could her father have let the house go to pot like this? Didn't it mean anything to him?

But did she have a right to criticize anything her dad did or didn't do with any part of the ranch, after what she'd done? Still, she'd only been a teenager when she'd decided not to return to Wyoming; why on earth had her dad let her get away with such bratty behavior?

Carly sighed. She knew why Stuart had let her get away with anything and everything while growing up. It was because her mother had died when she'd been too young to remember, and her father had tried to make it up to her.

The old house tugged at Carly's heartstrings as she walked through the first floor rooms and realized that the place wasn't even clean. There were huge dust motes in corners and under furniture, and from the musty odor she was noticing she would bet anything that the windows hadn't been opened for fresh air in ages.

"Obviously Banyon could live in a pigsty and not be bothered by it," she muttered as she entered the big old-fashioned kitchen. Positive that the refrigerator would contain moldy food, if any, she pulled open the door, then stood there and blinked at the laden shelves. And it was fresh food she was seeing, too, fresh milk, meat and vegetables.

"Odd," she mumbled, staring at the array. Surely Banyon hadn't gone out of his way to provide this food for her, had he? Of course, her dad might have asked him to stock the kitchen, just in case she would rather eat alone than with the men. Yes, that was something Stuart would think of doing. She certainly couldn't imagine Banyon doing it without a nudge.

After checking the refrigerator for bottled water and finding none, Carly shut the door and went to locate a glass for a drink of tap water, which she doubted was drinkable, but what choice did she have?

The sink water was cold and delicious, and Carly stood at a window and had her drink. Something began niggling her; more than likely she had let her dad down by arguing with Banyon almost from the moment they'd set eyes on each other.

But how could she not have spoken her mind about that stallion? Shooting him would be a terrible crime, and she still felt that she would stop at nothing to see that it didn't happen.

She would like to discuss this with her father and find out for herself how he felt about it, but wouldn't that be a lot like tattling? Frowning, Carly decided that whatever problems she might have with Jake or his methods of operating the ranch during her stay, she should not cause a breach between Banyon and her father. Their relationship had worked very well for at least four years, and she'd been on the ranch no more than a half hour and already she could stir up trouble with a few words to her dad. She couldn't let that happen. It would be unjustifiably selfish of her to let that happen, especially in light of the promises she'd made herself during the past year to not cause her father any more headaches.

Sighing heavily, Carly headed for the staircase to the second floor. She might as well pick a bedroom for herself. Someone would probably be bringing in her luggage at any moment.

Halfway up the stairs she went back down and found a telephone. Dialing her father's private number, she left a message on his voice mail: "Hi, Dad, it's me. I'm at the ranch and everything is fine. Hope your business trip to London is going well, though you probably only just got there. Anyway, call if and when you want, though don't feel it's necessary. We'll talk when you have the time. Love you. Bye."

Three

Jake was sorely disappointed and more than a little angry. The two men who'd spotted the stallion, then chased him, had quite a story to tell when Jake finally met up with them shortly before suppertime.

"We'd a caught him for sure if that danged helicopter hadn't spooked our horses," Artie Campbell said disgustedly.

"We would've, Jake," Joe Franklin agreed. "In two seconds flat that devil was in the woods. We followed, but it was a waste of time. He can race through trees and underbrush faster than greased lightning."

"Did you happen to spot any of our mares?" Jake spoke stiffly, because his entire body was stiff. Losing the stallion today was Carly Paxton's fault. Jake had put two and two together about the helicopter veering just before landing. Carly had noticed the men chasing the stallion and had wanted a closer look. The pilot, of course, had merely done as she'd asked.

"Not a one of 'em," Artie said. "He must have 'em hid out somewhere."

Jake nodded grimly. "Okay, you men did your best today. Maybe we'll have better luck the next time he shows himself. I'm going to go clean up for supper. See you later."

Heading for the house, Jake battled the irritation and resentment prickling his system. Carly Paxton was a royal pain in the neck. There was a darned good chance of that rogue stallion having been captured today. Without Carly's nosiness, that thieving horse might be installed in an escape-proof steel pen right now, and Jake could be trying to figure out what to do with him instead of cursing the frustration gnawing a hole in his gut.

Entering the house by the back door, Jake paused in the kitchen to cool down his temper. As much as he'd like to lambaste Carly for her role in this afternoon's fiasco with the stallion, he had to treat her cordially. The situation galled Jake, but he was stuck with it. Stuck with that woman on the ranch for only God knew how long.

Jake sighed heavily. If she wasn't Stuart's daughter...

But therein lay the bind. She *was* Stuart's daughter, and already he'd snapped at her and even let her think he would shoot that stallion just because she had annoyed him with her questions. He'd better shape up and be nice, however much it went against his grain. Snorting disgustedly, Jake left the kitchen, took a quick look through the first-floor rooms in case Carly was downstairs, then headed for the second floor.

There were four large bedrooms up there—including the one he used—and he started knocking on doors and calling, "Carly?"

She was still unpacking, hanging clothes in the closet and putting other things in bureau drawers, when she heard Jake's voice. Going to the door of the room she'd chosen, she opened it. "Yes?" she said coolly.

Jake tried very hard to smile, to appear relaxed and congenial. "Did you get settled in?"

"I'm working on it."

Looking into her beautiful green eyes made Jake nervous, and he averted his gaze and resented Carly for unnerving him in such a personal way. Certainly he was still angry with her, but deep down he knew that anger was not the cause of his present discomfort. He didn't want to be attracted to a woman he just barely knew and thus far didn't much care for, but there were sparks in his body that were undeniably sexual. It might have been a while for him, but the signs of physical attraction were never really forgotten, even if a man strove diligently to forget a past he'd be better off not having.

Shying from such discomfiting thoughts, Jake uneasily shifted his weight from one foot to the other and cleared his throat. "Uh, there are a few things I should've told you about when you first got here."

He seemed unduly uncomfortable to Carly, but she didn't feel particularly kindly toward him and she felt no sympathy at all for this overbearing man. "Tell me now," she said without a trace of warmth or friendliness.

"Yes, thanks, I will. I stocked the kitchen with groceries, in case you wanted to avoid taking your meals with the men. You're welcome to eat in the men's dining room, of course, but that's up to you. Incidentally, Barney, the cook, will be ringing the dinner bell in about—" Jake checked his watch "—fifteen minutes."

"Dad told me the same thing about meals. Thank you for providing groceries." Thanking him was an automatic reflex. Carly believed she had Banyon pretty much figured out: he was *only* putting up with her because she was his boss's daughter. Jake had out-and-out lied when he'd told her that she was no intrusion at all. He didn't like her being here, and he was, naturally, trying to conceal how he really felt about it.

"You're welcome. The other thing I forgot to mention when you arrived was transportation. There's a car in the garage you can use when you want. The keys are hanging on a hook in the kitchen—easy to find—and…''

Carly cut in. ''Is it your car?''

''No, it's yours. I mean, your dad bought it and…''

She broke in again. ''Then it belongs to the ranch. I'll be happy to use it with one condition. If you need it you'll tell me so I don't go off someday and leave you stranded.''

Jake frowned. Maybe she really didn't intend to intrude and have everything her way while she was here. Her attitude on the car was decent and unselfish, even though he rarely drove it and she could call it her own during her visit.

''Well, that's about it,'' he said lamely. ''See you later.''

Not tonight, you won't! Since there was food in the kitchen, she would prepare her own dinner and eat alone. She was in no mood to dine with a bunch of strangers, especially male strangers. Truth was, she didn't like men very much anymore. Her ex had really done a number on her, and if one man on this ranch leered at her, or even tried to flirt with her, she was apt to smack him.

Shutting the door after Jake had gone, she went to a window and looked out. She might not like its manager, but she could find no fault with the ranch itself. Other than the house, that is, which, if nothing else, needed a good cleaning.

But the area was quiet, peaceful and scenically beautiful. Maybe her dad had been right to suggest that she spend some time here.

Her blood stirred suddenly. However tranquil this place appeared to be, it had disturbing aspects. One, at least, that wild stallion. Had she spoken her mind clearly enough on that subject to make Banyon understand that he or any of his men had better not shoot that horse?

Agitated again, Carly knew she would not rest until she was positive that Banyon had taken her seriously. The mere idea of deliberately killing a healthy horse was appalling and she simply was not going to stand for it.

Marching from her bedroom, she went to the door of

Jake's room and knocked loudly. It opened after a minute, and she was startled to see Banyon dripping water and wearing nothing but a towel around his lower half.

Her heart sank. She should have figured out that he'd been planning on taking a shower before dinner and she most certainly should *not* have put them both in this embarrassing situation.

"Uh, sorry," she stammered, looking everywhere but at him. Still, the look she'd gotten when he'd opened the door was etched on her brain. He was, without a doubt, the sexiest-looking guy she'd ever set eyes on.

She began backing away. "Sorry I—I disturbed you. I was going, uh, going to tell you something, but it…it can wait."

Holding the towel together at his waist, Jake stepped into the hall. "Wait a minute! If you have something to tell me, go ahead and say it."

She couldn't do it, not with him half-naked and stirring feelings within her that she had wholeheartedly believed were dead and buried.

"Tomorrow," she called over her shoulder as she hastened down the hall to her own bedroom. "I'll talk to you tomorrow." With her heart thumping hard, she closed the door behind herself. "Damn," she whispered, terribly shaken over that little scene. How could she have been so dense as to not realize that he'd come to the house to clean up for dinner?

Jake stood in the hall until her bedroom door closed, wondering what that had been all about. Then he glanced down at himself and couldn't help chuckling. Obviously his opening his bedroom door wearing just a towel had disoriented Carly, which seemed pretty funny until he visualized *her* opening her door half-naked.

The amusement faded from his system, and, scowling darkly, he reentered his bedroom and shut the door. The next time someone came to his room unexpectedly he'd damned well better remember who it was that could be doing the knocking.

* * *

Hordes of people paraded through Carly's dreams that night—her ex-husband, many of her friends and…Jake Banyon. All the dreams were disturbing, but the one about Jake was the worst; he wasn't wearing even a towel in that dream, he was stark naked!

Carly awoke in a sweat, practically gasping for air. She jumped out of bed and ran to the window she'd opened before retiring, where she sucked in huge breaths of cool night air. She was *not* attracted to Jake Banyon, she told herself, she wasn't! Dreaming of him naked was perverted. What was wrong with her?

"Oh, no," she whispered as the details of that dream became much too clear in her mind. Banyon had been fully aroused and walking toward her with shadowed eyes, and she'd been on fire and…and…

Groaning, she covered her face with her hands. Why on earth would her brain devise such an erotic dream about a man she didn't even like?

The next day, dressed in jeans and boots, with her long hair arranged in a single braid, Carly hiked around the compound, peering into barns and other outbuildings, and generally getting acquainted with the lay of the land. She found the garage and the car Jake had told her to use if she wanted, and she tried to picture him driving an ordinary car and found it hard to do. From what she'd seen of him so far, pickups and sports utility models seemed more his style. Instinct told her that his machismo was neither forced nor phony. He was so typically the western male—as portrayed in movies and novels, she thought cynically—that there was no way she could place him in any other scenario.

Moving on, she realized that there were no men about—not even one of the ranch hands. She stopped at a corral to pet a pretty palomino mare's nose and thought of taking a ride. The mare seemed gentle and responsive to her voice and caresses, and being on a horse seemed like a wonderful way to spend a few hours.

But where were the saddles kept? There must be a tack room in one of the barns, she decided, and headed for the nearest one.

She was almost there when she heard music. She stopped to listen closer so she could determine where it was coming from. Her gaze swept the compound.

"The cookhouse," she whispered, and veered from the barn to investigate that building. Inside was a large dining room, with numerous tables and chairs. She walked through that room to the kitchen and stopped in the doorway. An older man wearing a white apron was peeling potatoes at the sink.

"Barney?" she said.

He turned around and grinned. "Ms. Paxton?"

Smiling, Carly walked in and offered her hand. "I can't tell you how many times I've heard Dad praise your cooking."

Barney hastily turned down the radio, wiped his palm on his apron and heartily shook her hand. "That's real nice to hear, ma'am, real nice. Your pa is a real nice gent, real nice."

"Yes, he is, Barney, and please call me Carly."

"Thank you, ma'am, I'll do that."

Carly had to smile again. "It smells very good in here."

"That's cause I've got some cakes in the oven. Uh, everyone knows you arrived yesterday, but what did you do, eat alone in that big empty house last night?"

"Yes, I really didn't feel like company."

"Well, tell you what. Anytime you don't want company at mealtime, you just come to the kitchen and I'll prepare a nice plate you can take to the house. You don't even have to walk through the dining room, if you don't want to. As you can see, the kitchen has its own door."

"That's very kind, Barney, thank you. I'll probably take you up on that offer."

"Anytime, ma'am, anytime."

"Well, I know you're busy. It was good meeting you, Barney."

"My pleasure, ma'am."

Carly started out, then stopped. "Barney, do you know the name of the palomino in the big corral?"

"Sure, that's Goldie. Pretty thing, ain't she?"

"Very. Well, I'll let you get back to work." Carly exited by the kitchen door. Barney was a dear, and Carly felt good because there was at least one person on the ranch she could talk to without worrying about how he might take what she said. That thought bothered her. Was she really worried over how Banyon might take anything she said?

"Not on your life," she mumbled under her breath. Banyon might be the top dog in these parts, but he didn't daunt her one little bit.

Even when he's half-naked? A tingle went up Carly's spine at the image that question provoked, and she tensed her lips in self-annoyance. That man was not going to get to her, not if he walked around completely naked, damn his arrogant hide!

Quick-stepping to the large barn again, Carly went inside and located the tack room. It was a beautiful day, and she wasn't going to waste it by puttering in the house. There were a number of saddles on racks, and she picked one and carried it out to the corral. The golden mare was as gentle as Carly had thought and stood quite still while Carly put first a blanket, then the saddle, on her back.

Leading Goldie from the corral Carly mounted, and it was a marvelous sensation to be on horseback again. Exhilarated, Carly nudged the mare into a walk and headed for open country.

Jake and three of his men returned to the compound around noon. The others had their lunches with them, as they were moving cattle from one pasture to another in the southernmost portion of the ranch.

Riding up to the main corral near the largest barn, Jake pulled his horse to a halt and frowned. "Did someone move Goldie to another corral?" he asked.

All three men looked blank. One of them finally said, "Not that I know of, Jake," and the other two agreed.

Jake looked at that empty corral and felt a discomfiting premonition in his gut. But it was a premonition without definition, and he honestly didn't know what was causing it, except for the fact that he hadn't asked anyone to move Goldie and someone had. Goldie was a valuable horse and she was in season. Jake had put her in this particular corral so he could keep a close eye on her. He'd been planning to mate her with Caesar, a pale blond thoroughbred stallion, when the time was right.

"Jake, maybe that wild stallion stole her," one of the men said. "He's getting bolder all the time. Maybe he came right into the compound this morning and stole Goldie while everyone was gone."

Startled by that idea, Jake studied the high pole fencing of the corral and tried to visualize Goldie, or any other horse on the place, having enough space in the enclosure to get up enough speed to jump the fence. Mares in season and stallions accomplished remarkable feats to get to each other, but clearing that high fence from a short distance would be more than remarkable. It would be damn near impossible.

"I don't think so," Jake finally said. "I'm going to go and talk to Barney. Maybe he knows something." Hurrying off toward the cookhouse, he heard the three men exchanging ideas about what might have happened to Goldie. None of their theories seemed feasible to Jake, and he closed his ears to them.

Entering the cookhouse kitchen, he got right to the point. "Barney, did you happen to hear anything unusual this morning?"

"Unusual? Like what, Jake?"

"Goldie's not in her corral. Did any of the men come back

and maybe move her? Not that anyone should've moved her, but something happened to her.''

Barney shook his head. "No one came back that I know of, Jake, and I didn't hear anything unusual. Course, I had been playing my radio, you know.''

"Okay, thanks.'' Jake started to leave.

"Oh, wait a minute, Jake. Carly Paxton dropped in and chatted a few minutes. Real nice lady, she is, real nice. Just like her pa. Anyway, she asked me if I knew the name of the palomino horse in the corral. I told her, of course.''

Jake felt such a strong sinking sensation that his knees got weak. "Did she say anything about taking Goldie for a ride?''

"Nope, not a thing. Jake...Jake? What about some lunch?'' Barney called as Jake ran out.

"We'll eat later,'' Jake yelled over his shoulder. He ran all the way to the house, hit the back door hard and then ran through the rooms like a whirlwind, shouting Carly's name. When it was obvious she wasn't on the first floor, he took the stairs to the second floor two and three at a time, rushed down the hall and unceremoniously pushed open her bedroom door.

"Damn you!'' he yelled when he saw nothing but a vacant bedroom. If that woman didn't prove to be the death of him this summer, it would be a miracle!

Retracing his steps at high speed, he ran back outside to the three men, who were still discussing Goldie's mysterious disappearance. When they saw Jake's dark and forbidding expression, they fell silent.

"I want the three of you to go and find the other men. Then all of you are to spread out and look for Carly Paxton and Goldie. I'm positive Carly took Goldie for a ride.''

"Hell's bells,'' one of the men muttered. "Don't she know Goldie's in heat? If that stallion gets wind of Goldie, no telling what might happen.''

Jake's expression became even darker. "Let's get going,''

he said gruffly, climbing onto his own horse. He had no idea in which direction to even start looking for Carly and Goldie, but he couldn't just stand around and worry.

On horseback, the four men tore out of the compound.

Goldie behaves like a lady, Carly thought, extremely pleased with herself over having thought of taking this marvelous ride. The open fields, bright from sunlight, were lovely with wildflowers and birds flying this way and that. The grazing cattle paid her no mind, and Carly felt a wonderful sense of serenity that had been missing from her life for too long a time.

Her dad had been very wise to suggest she come here, she thought with a feeling of love for Stuart Paxton. As she rode, Carly vowed once more to never worry him again and couldn't help recalling that he had warned her against marrying Burke Stenson. The Stenson family was as financially well-off as the Paxtons, but Burke's personal reputation had concerned Stuart.

"He's a gambler, Carly. Please don't think you can change him," Stuart had said.

But she'd been madly in love and hadn't heeded a word said to her about Burke. It was the only time in her life that she had openly defied her father, and she had lived to regret it. Burke hadn't just been a gambler. In fact, that had been his good side, and she probably could have lived with it. But Burke had also been emotionally and physically abusive, and she had not been able to live with black eyes, a bruised body and a shattered heart for long. Her marriage had lasted three years, and looking back at the misery of it she wondered why she'd stayed *that* long.

Carly pushed that phase of her life from her mind because she hated thinking about it. Besides, if she was going to attempt some serious thinking, it should be about what she intended to do when she returned to New York. Before her marriage she had worked in advertising, and it was a career she could go back to, she knew. She just hadn't found her way yet, but she would.

But she didn't want to be serious today, not about anything, and she rode through grassy fields, moving farther and farther away from the compound, thinking scattered thoughts and even doing some humming, simply because it was a fabulous day and she felt so carefree on that beautiful mare's back.

Approaching a series of foothills, Goldie suddenly tossed her head and whinnied, startling Carly out of her insouciant mood. She patted the mare's neck and murmured calming words, but the pretty mare still seemed agitated.

"What is it, girl?" Carly asked quietly, looking around to see what might have alarmed the horse. A snake, maybe? Remembering that her father had said there were rattlesnakes in certain areas of the ranch, Carly anxiously searched the ground. She saw nothing but grass and a tiny field mouse running for its hole. A mouse shouldn't spook Goldie, but then she really didn't know the mare that well, did she?

Carly urged Goldie to move on, and the mare obeyed. Carly relaxed again. The foothills looked interesting. She could see pine trees and thought she heard the movement of water, a creek perhaps. Goldie could have a drink, Carly thought as she urged the mare up a hill and into the trees.

Oh, this is lovely. It was much cooler in the trees, and the sound of the creek was louder. Wondering if she, too, could have drink from a creek, if it was safe for a human to drink from a creek, Carly realized that she should have brought some water with her. She would not forget water the next time she took a ride, she told herself.

Well, she would let Goldie have a drink, then start back. In the next breath her heart nearly stopped beating. Not twenty feet away, directly in her path, was the black stallion she'd seen from the helicopter yesterday. He was as physically magnificent as she'd thought then, but he didn't look very friendly, and Carly's mouth was suddenly drier than it had been a minute ago.

The stallion pawed the ground, threw his head around and snorted. Goldie began prancing around, throwing *her* head around and whinnying softly.

"Oh, my God," Carly whispered as fear shot through her. The stallion wanted to add Goldie to his harem, and the mare was responding to his call!

The stallion reared and his whinny sounded like a scream. Stunned and scared to death, Carly tried to calm Goldie, but the mare, in her present state of excitement, was far more horse than Carly could handle. Goldie reared to her hind legs, and Carly tried desperately to hang on, but the next thing she knew she had hit the ground, hard.

The last thing Carly saw before passing out was Goldie running off after the stallion.

Four

Carly was unconscious only a few minutes. When her eyes opened, she stared up at the patch of blue sky visible through the trees and realized that she was almost afraid of getting to her feet, or of trying to. If she'd broken a bone in that fall, what would she do?

With a rapid heartbeat borne of dread, Carly gingerly began testing the mobility of her own body. It was relieving to be able to move her arms and legs with no more than the discomfort of a few aches and pains. Cautiously, she got up from the ground, then clung to a small tree until the dizziness in her head passed. She analyzed what had happened: the fall from Goldie's back, so unexpected and startling, had knocked the wind out of her and was the reason she'd passed out.

Her pragmatic side accepted the analysis and began wondering how far she was from the ranch compound and how long it would take her to walk back to it. She believed that she knew the right direction in which to start walking, but then she felt a spurt of uneasiness when she glanced around and everything looked the same.

That way, she thought, then changed her mind. No, that way. If she weren't in the trees, if she'd stayed in open country...

She sucked in a long, suddenly nervous breath. She might as well face facts. The fall had disoriented her; she didn't know which way to go to get out of the trees! One thing kept her from panicking: she'd only been riding in the pine forest for twenty minutes or so. She checked the time on her wristwatch. If she walked for twenty minutes, in any direction, and saw nothing but more trees, she would turn around and try another direction.

Yes, that made sense. Keeping track of the time would be crucial, and she would mark this spot so she could recognize it if and when she had to return to it to maintain her bearings.

Ignoring the aches in her body, Carly let go of the tree, located three rocks that she stacked in a pile—surely she would recognize those rocks if she saw them again—and then set out walking.

By four that afternoon Jake was in a sweat. His path had crossed that of his men several times in their search, and no one had found even a clue as to Carly's whereabouts.

He had reorganized the search at one point, telling some members of his crew to return to the compound and exchange their horses for pickup trucks. There were a lot of roads crisscrossing the ranch, and each and every one of them should be checked.

But he stuck to his horse, because the terrain of the vast ranch was so varied and much of it could only be reached on horseback. Peering into deep canyons and crevices was unnerving for Jake, because he was beginning to fear that Carly had run into trouble. His most consoling thought was that she had merely gotten lost and was aimlessly—and probably frighteningly—attempting to find her way back to the compound.

At moments, though, while riding and searching, Jake felt a searing anger. How dare she take a horse she knew nothing about and go off the way she had? She at least could have told Barney what she'd intended doing. Barney would have warned her against riding Goldie, and this whole thing would not have happened. If Carly was safe and sound when someone finally found her, Jake was going to give her hell in no uncertain terms, and she could call her dad and tattle or do anything else she felt like doing about it.

Around five Jake found himself near the foothills. He stopped his horse and frowned at the pine forests darkening the hills. Was Carly dumb enough to get herself lost in the forests? Jake's heart sank. If she was in those trees, it could take days to find her. He glanced up at the sun; he still had two hours of full daylight and about another hour of fading light as the sun went down.

And then the thought that he'd been trying to keep at bay for hours would remain buried no longer: if Carly had run into that stallion she could be seriously injured, or even worse. The idea of phoning Stuart with that sort of news was so chilling that Jake couldn't let himself dwell on it. Kicking his horse in the ribs, he headed up the nearest hill toward the pine trees.

Carly had returned to her little pile of rocks more times than she cared to count, and she'd had to start battling a developing fear. She was exhausted and had to rest awhile before trying yet another direction. She sat down with her back against a tree and shut her eyes.

She was so angry with herself that she could think of nothing else. *You fool, you moron. How could you have gotten yourself into a mess like this? No one at the ranch has probably even missed you. All the men were out working when you left, and they're probably still out on the range!*

But when they did get back, wouldn't someone notice that Goldie was gone? Surely Banyon was smart enough to figure out that she'd taken the palomino for a ride.

God, what an idiot she was! The mare was obviously in season and giving off that special scent that drove stallions wild, and he was a wild thing to begin with. He'd picked up Goldie's scent and come after her, bold and unafraid of the human on the mare's back. Goldie had gotten rid of her burden to follow that handsome brute, as easily as if Carly had been a sack of potatoes. And Carly would bet anything that Banyon would have plenty to say about this whole fiasco when she was finally back at the compound.

If she was ever back at the compound, that is. Tears suddenly coursed down Carly's cheeks. The afternoon was almost gone. Night would be falling soon, and she was out here all alone, hungry, thirsty and hurting. She'd never been afraid of the dark, but then she'd never put in a night in a black forest, either. Were there animals out here? Bears or wolves? Her ignorance of this untamed country was both maddening and frightening.

Listlessly she wiped her tear-streaked face on the sleeve of her blouse. She had to try walking in another direction; she couldn't just sit here and wait for nightfall and for some voracious animal to decide she would make a good meal.

She was halfway to her feet when she heard something. Dear Lord, was it a voice? Yes, there it was again! Someone was shouting her name!

"I'm here," she shrieked as loudly as she could.

"Carly?" the voice yelled again.

"Over here!"

"Carly?"

"Yes! Yes!"

"Stay put!"

"I will!" Her knees almost buckled in relief, but she stayed on her feet and clung to the tree for support.

Jake finally spotted her through the trees, and he, too, was so relieved that he got weak. Carly was standing, so she apparently wasn't injured. Thank God for that. Goldie was nowhere to be seen, though, and Jake's lips thinned as the weakness in his system vanished and was replaced by one of the blackest rages of his life. He knew instantly what had happened, as surely as if he'd witnessed it for himself. That rogue stallion had stolen Goldie right from under Carly's seat; one more of the ranch's best mares was now a member of that devil's harem!

When Carly saw who her rescuer was, she instantly became defensive. She didn't expect Banyon to be nice about this. And even though she might deserve anything he said to her, she wasn't going to meekly accept a dressing-down.

"Are you okay?" Jake gruffly asked while dismounting.

She wouldn't admit to feeling like one huge toothache to Banyon for love nor money, and knowing that he had to see the remnants of tears on her face, she would give anything not to have cried. "I'm fine," she said curtly while ignoring his angry scowl.

"I'm glad you're all right, but I'm not even going to try to stop myself from telling you how I feel about what you did today. First of all, you set the whole damn ranch on end. Everyone is still out looking for you, and no one's had a decent meal since morning. What in hell makes you think you can just go off by yourself without letting someone know? And taking Goldie for a ride was the most stupid thing you could have done. Now she's gone, isn't she? You ran into that stallion, and she dumped you and went with him. She's worth at least fifty thousand dollars, and there's a damn good chance of never getting her back. I wonder how your dad will take that news."

"My dad will be relieved I wasn't seriously injured, you jerk! Unlike you, money isn't the only thing he thinks of!"

"If money was all I thought of, no one would've come looking for you, you spoiled brat! Now, get on the back of my horse and let's get the hell out of here. While you rest

and pamper yourself at the ranch, I'm going to have to round
up the men and tell them I found you. It'll probably take me
half the night.''

"I hope it takes you *all* night!" Carly was angry enough
to slap his surly face. "You might know how to run this
ranch, but you're the most inconsiderate, overbearing person
I've ever known. Dad doesn't know that, though, does he?
With him you're always sweet as pie. Well, let me tell you
something, *Mister* Banyon. My father might be an easygoing
guy, but sooner or later he'll catch on to your true colors,
you big phony!"

Her fury shocked Jake. He was not a phony anything, dammit, and how dare she call him names and act as though none
of this was her fault? He should have let her spend the night
alone in these woods; she wouldn't be so quick to harangue
a rescuer by morning.

His face turned to granite. "Shut the hell up and get on
my horse. With or without you, I'm leaving."

She believed him. From the cold, stony expression on his
face she wouldn't dare *not* believe him. In fact, he looked as
though he would just love to ride off without her, leaving
her to God knew what fate.

Still, her spirit wasn't entirely destroyed, and she shot him
a look of pure venom before releasing her grip on the tree.
It hadn't entered her mind that she might have a problem
with walking over to his horse, but her legs gave out on her
third step and she nearly took another fall. Teetering, she
reached out for something, and the only thing there was Banyon. He grabbed her and held her upright.

"Why didn't you say you were injured?" he growled,
sounding like an enraged bear.

His arms around her felt like solid security, but his accusing attitude was intolerable.

"I'm just a little weak," she said sharply. "Just help me
get on your horse, and I'll be fine."

Holding her was doing peculiar things to Jake. She'd been

trouble from the moment she'd arrived, he suspected she would continue to disrupt his life until the day she left the ranch, and she still felt incredibly sensuous in his arms. Her breasts, full and soft, against his chest clouded his mind and demolished his anger. He suddenly wanted to kiss her, and without thinking such rash behavior through, he brought his mouth down on hers.

Carly's gasp of surprise got hung up in her throat, and she realized how defenseless she was right then. She'd pretty much depleted her normal reserve of strength, and even if Jake's arms weren't pinning hers to her sides, how could she break free when she had so little energy?

More startling than the initial shock of being kissed, though, was the almost instantaneous response of her body. A most incredible thrill started at the back of her neck and moved down from there, finally whirling hotly in the pit of her stomach.

But Carly's sense of shock was no more severe or strained than Jake's. He had not expected to feel such an explosion of desire, nor emotions so long denied they'd been all but forgotten. One little kiss should not tear a man apart, and that was how he felt, as though he was being ripped from stem to stern. It scared him, and he was so damned disappointed in himself for even touching Carly that he became queasy.

Concealing everything he felt behind a stony expression, he raised his head. "Sorry," he growled. "That was a mistake."

Carly's eyes widened. He had enjoyed kissing her—they had both liked it, wise or not—and it galled her that he would apologize so cavalierly about something that was still affecting her. She simply could not let him have the last word, not on this, she couldn't!

"Just make sure it doesn't happen again," she snapped heatedly.

Jake felt a flush creep up his neck to his face. To cover his embarrassment he fell back on anger. "You're not irresistible, so don't let your imagination run wild," he snarled. "Come on, let's get you on my horse." He surprised Carly into another gasp—this one audible—when he bent a little and scooped her up from the ground.

"I can walk!" she screeched.

"Do me a favor and shut up!" Carrying Carly, Jake headed for his horse.

That was twice he'd told her to shut up, and it was one time too many. "I will *not* shut up," she said furiously. "I'll speak my mind anytime, anyplace. You don't scare me, so you might as well stop trying to."

Jake was seething again. "I'm not trying to scare you, you little fool." He heaved her up onto the back of his horse, putting her just behind the saddle.

"You're a bigger fool than I am, any day of the week." It was an inane comeback, but it was the only one Carly could think of.

"And you're an ingrate."

"I'm not ungrateful, but you gave me no chance at all to say thanks! You attacked me the second you rode up!" *And you kissed me! How dare you kiss me like I belonged to you and then act like it never happened?*

"With damn good reason," Jake snarled as he swung himself up into the saddle and picked up the reins. "Hang on to me."

At that moment she would rather suffer a lonely death in the woods after dark than touch him, but there was no other handhold, and, gritting her teeth, she gingerly laid her hands on each side of his torso.

"You'd better hang on tighter than that, or you could find yourself sliding down the rump of this horse and landing on your own rump." Jake clucked his tongue and got the horse moving.

Carly wanted to put Banyon in his place in the worst way, but exhaustion and pain were catching up with her. She wasn't even hungry or thirsty now. All she could think of was crawling into bed, closing her eyes and permitting herself to fall asleep. She could sleep right now, she realized with her head nodding. She fought the sensation for as long as she could, then she gave up and let her forehead fall forward to Banyon's strong back.

Jake felt her head against his back and got very tense. For four years he'd lived a good clean life, and no one would ever convince him that he would have been able to turn the hell-bent course he'd been on if he hadn't gotten away completely from women. Now one had invaded his territory, and she was reminding him much too clearly that there were few earthly joys in living like a monk. Besides, this territory wasn't really Jake's, it was Carly's dad's, and other than quitting his job, the mere thought of which nearly destroyed Jake, there wasn't anything he could do to avoid her. As painful as it was to admit, if only to himself, he wished they were still back in that clearing, making wild, crazy love. Jake's lips thinned angrily, because he was thinking of sex now, and that, too, was Carly Paxton's fault.

And then, for some reason, he started regretting yelling at her. He could have handled this whole thing a lot more tactfully. Yes, she had caused the loss of a valuable mare. And yes, she was driving him crazy with erotic thoughts. But she was green as a gourd in this country, and he hadn't had to be so harsh with her. It would have been far better—in more ways than one—if he'd immediately gotten her on his horse and taken her back to the compound. Then, the following day, he could have talked to her in a sane and sensible way about how badly impulsive behavior could turn out in this isolated wilderness, especially on a ranch of this size. Actually, it was a miracle that he'd found her before dark.

Jake walked his horse because of its double load, and long before they reached the compound he felt Carly's full weight against his back. Apparently she'd given up on maintaining some distance between their bodies, undoubtedly because of her exhaustion, and again he felt the incredible pressure of her soft breasts.

"Damn," he whispered, and sucked in a shaky breath. He

had to face the truth, like it or not. Carly made him ache. He
wanted to lay his boss's daughter down in the grass, undress
her and…and…

"And not just one time," he mumbled. Almost at once
denial exploded in his system. He wasn't going to lay any
woman down in the grass, dammit, but he especially was not
going to make that kind of pass at his boss's daughter. A
kiss had been bad enough. What had happened to him when
Carly stepped off that helicopter? Had he lost his mind over
the first pretty woman he'd been forced to talk to in four
years?

Disgusted with his suddenly active libido, Jake berated
himself for the rest of the ride. Nothing was going to happen
between him and Carly, by damn, not one thing that she
couldn't tell her dad about. The next time he saw Stuart, he
was going to be able to look him straight in the eye, as he'd
always done.

Because he, too, was bone-tired and hungry, Jake was glad
when the long ride was over. He said quietly, "We're home,
Carly."

She stirred and mumbled, "Home?"

"We're at the compound. I'm going to get down first, then
help you down. Hang onto the saddle."

Only half-awake, she followed his orders like an automaton. She let him take her by the waist and lift her from the
horse's back, and she made not a peep of objection when he
picked her up and carried her into the house and upstairs to
her bedroom.

She vaguely registered being put on the bed and was already sound asleep when Jake laid a blanket over her.

He looked at her for a heart-wrenching moment, regretting
again how harshly he'd dealt with her mistake in judgment,
then felt his mood change abruptly from regret to desire
again. Laden with sexual tension again, he practically ran
from her room.

Carly slept through the night and half of the following
morning. She was stiff and sore when she finally forced her-

self out of bed, but a hot bath and a couple of over-the-counter pain pills helped, and she managed to get dressed with only a modicum of discomfort.

In a way yesterday seemed a bit unreal. Until she recalled Banyon's anger and then his kiss, that is. Those things had been very real, and it raised her hackles every time she thought about either of them. He had no right to kiss her, and what in the devil had gotten into him? But neither did he have the right to speak to her the way he had, and she would never forgive him for calling her a spoiled brat. If he hoped that the animosity between them was going to make her leave the ranch, he had another thought coming. She was going to stay for as long as she wanted, and he could like it or lump it. In fact, she relished the idea of her presence driving him up the wall. If ever there was a man who needed to be taken down a peg or two, it was Jake Banyon, the arrogant jerk.

Carly went downstairs and made herself some breakfast. After eating, she sipped a second cup of coffee and looked out the kitchen window at the compound. Not a man was in sight. Obviously Banyon had his crew out on the range again.

Carly sighed. The silence of the house felt oppressive. What was she going to do all day?

Take a drive, a voice in her head said, and Carly nodded. Yes, a drive around the area and maybe to Tamarack, the nearest town, would cheer her up.

Quickly she rinsed the dishes she'd used and placed them in the dishwasher. She easily located the keys to the car in the garage, then went upstairs for her purse.

She was outside, on her way to the garage, when she remembered Banyon's railing at her for not letting someone know where she'd gone yesterday. As much as she resented the man and his imperious attitude, she had unpleasant first-hand experience with impulsive behavior.

Fine, she thought with righteous indignation. Even though it went against her grain to report in like a wayward child, she would tell Barney that she was taking the car for a drive. Changing directions, she walked to the cookhouse and went in through the kitchen door.

Barney smiled at her. "How are you this morning?"

"I'm fine, Barney, thank you for asking."

"Well, everyone was real worried about you yesterday. We're all mighty relieved today, I can tell you."

For the first time Carly felt genuine remorse over yesterday's misadventure. "I'm sorry that I worried anyone, Barney," she said quietly. "I promise it won't happen again."

"You got a real good look at that stallion, didn't you? Probably scared you to death, but I'm real curious about him. What does he look like, close up?"

"He's the most magnificent horse I've ever seen. His black hide looks smooth as silk, and when he reared to his hind legs, his muscles rippled like ocean currents. He's beautiful, Barney, that's really the best word to describe him."

"Well, I might just get a look at him myself. Jake took all the men out to track him. Jake thinks now that the stallion's stomping ground is somewhere in the foothills. Jake would do just about anything to get our mares back, especially Goldie."

Carly's heart skipped a beat. Did "anything" include shooting the stallion? Panic suddenly rose in Carly's throat. She had to do something! Taking a drive was out now. She would not enjoy sight-seeing with this on her mind.

"Barney, I should have asked you yesterday and didn't, but I'm asking you now. Is there a horse that's safe for me to take for a ride?"

Barney looked surprised. "You wanna take another ride today? Aren't you all staved up from that fall yesterday?"

"Only a little."

"Well…there are geldings in the horse pasture," Barney said slowly, conveying reluctance in imparting such information.

"Which is where?" Barney's disapproval was obvious, but Carly wasn't looking for anyone's approval. If there was any chance at all of her stopping Banyon from shooting that stallion, she had to take it.

"Out behind the smallest barn. Ma'am, I ain't sure you should be riding so soon after taking the tumble you did yesterday. And maybe you should tell me where you plan to go, just in case Jake comes in and wants to know."

"Barney, with any luck at all Jake will see me for himself."

"You're going after him?" Barney was clearly astonished. "Ma'am, he's got a three-hour head-start on you. You'll never find him."

"Maybe not, but I have to try. Oh, do you have a canteen I can use for water?"

"Yes, but..." Barney looked as though he was wishing that she wasn't involving him in today's adventure, even with as simple a thing as providing her with a canteen.

"Please, Barney, give me the canteen," Carly said gently. She'd promised not to worry anyone on the ranch again, and five minutes later she was causing this kindly man to worry. "I'll be fine, Barney, really I will."

He frowned at her for a few moments, then went to a cupboard and took out a canteen. "If something happens to you today, Jake'll have my hide," Barney mumbled as he handed it to her.

"Nothing is going to go wrong today, Barney, I guarantee it." Holding up the canteen she said, "Thanks. See you later," then rushed from the cookhouse and hurried back to the house for some of the things she hadn't taken with her yesterday—a sandwich, a large straw hat to protect her face from the sun and, of course, water for the canteen.

Twenty minutes later she was on horseback again—today's horse was a spirited gray gelding with a sensitive mouth—and taking a direct route to the foothills.

If she was too late to prevent that stallion's death, or even if she never did locate Banyon and his men, she would have at least tried. There was some comfort in that knowledge.

Five

It thrilled Carly to locate the exact place in the pine forest where yesterday's incident with the stallion had taken place. Obviously she'd recovered her normal good sense of direction, which she'd lost temporarily after her fall from Goldie. Yes, she thought, there was her pile of three rocks—her landmark and probably what had saved her from wandering deeper into the woods.

And, as she had hoped, there were dozens of hoof marks all over the place. This spot had been Banyon's starting point in today's search for the stallion. It should be a simple matter to follow the tracks left by so many horses and eventually catch up with Jake and the crew.

Carly set out, reasoning that she would be traveling much faster than the men, because their trail was so obvious, while the one they would be attempting to follow, that of the stallion and Goldie, couldn't possibly be so clearly defined.

Still, a knot of anxiety in her midsection kept Carly tense. For all she knew, Jake or some of his men could be experi-

enced or professional trackers, and this was a brand-new occurrence for her. If they were moving as fast as she was,
there would always remain an unknown distance between
them. Unless they ran upon the stallion and stopped to do
their dirty work, that is.

No, don't even think that way, she told herself with a shudder. She *had* to stop them from killing that stallion; there was
no one else to do it.

Carly rode on, keeping a close eye on her direction and
any outstanding landmark she passed. She was determined
not to get lost today and have to deal with Banyon's derisive
anger again. She didn't doubt that he'd been relieved to find
her yesterday, but then he'd been so rude about it that she
might never forgive him.

Not that he'd give a damn, she thought cynically. Even
though he'd kissed her, Banyon obviously didn't like her,
which, when she thought about it, seemed odd. Friendship
with new acquaintances had never been a problem for her;
why on earth did she rub Jake Banyon so wrong?

Well, just as she'd said right to Banyon's face, she would
bet anything that he showed her father a much different side
of himself than he showed her. Stuart Paxton thought the sun
rose and set in Banyon's hind pocket, and often boasted
about the great ranch manager he had in Wyoming.

"He's really good at pulling the wool over your eyes,
Dad," Carly muttered, wondering if she shouldn't have a
long talk with her father about his "great" partner.

But that idea didn't set quite right with Carly. It was possible, after all, that Banyon had tried to like her and simply
couldn't make the grade, for some reason she couldn't
fathom, which, thinking rationally, had nothing at all to do
with his and her father's working arrangement. Of course, if
he honestly didn't like her, why had he kissed her?

Frowning, Carly pushed the subject from her thoughts. Up-
setting herself over Banyon's rudeness and unreasonable kiss

was silly when she had something as important and urgent
as that stallion's life to worry about.

The gelding she was riding obeyed her slightest command.
He was a marvelous horse, and Carly was pleased with herself for having picked him from the herd. Banyon should be
so malleable, she thought with a small snicker.

Her amusement vanished when she suddenly found herself
riding on small rocks—thousands of them! Frowning, Carly
pulled on the reins and stopped the horse. She checked her
watch: she'd been following the easily distinguishable tracks
left by Banyon and his men for two hours, then, without a
dram of warning, there were no tracks!

Where had the men gone from here? There were so many
smooth, small rocks, a long, winding swath of them, Carly
realized. Was she in a dry riverbed? That was what it looked
like.

What should she do now? She bit her lip while concentrating on the problem, then took a swallow of water from
her canteen. The gelding's head moved up and down, as
though he was urging her to make up her mind.

Okay, she thought. The men, too, had come to this old
riverbed, or whatever it was, and it wasn't likely they had
followed its course for long. She would ride the banks and
pick up their trail again.

An hour later she still hadn't found any trail *to* pick up,
and she was discouraged and worried. This setback in her
progress could mean the difference between life and death
for the stallion.

This needed some thought, she decided. She would dis-
mount, eat her sandwich and try to figure out a sensible next
move. For a few seconds she stared ahead, her gaze following
the swath of river rocks until it was swallowed by the terrain.
Then, frustrated by her own ignorance of tracking and reading trail signs, she directed her horse away from the rocks
and into the cooling shade of the timber. Dismounting, she
looped the reins securely around a solid little tree, took her

canteen of water and sandwich, then located a nice grassy spot in the midst of some trees to eat and do her thinking.

The sandwich was gone before she realized it; obviously she'd been hungry. After a drink of water, Carly leaned her back against a tree and tried to figure things out. Should she continue to follow the dry riverbed or just give up and return to the ranch? Today's excursion had to be construed as a failure. Heaven only knew where Banyon and his men had gone from here, and while Carly was beginning to learn her way around portions of the ranch, she wasn't yet confident enough to risk getting lost again.

Her head and eyes felt heavy; she had gotten very sleepy. Thinking that she would shut her eyes for just a few minutes, she slid down to the grass so that she was lying on her back, used her hat for a pillow and yawned. A short nap would revive her, she was certain.

The clatter of hooves on rocks awakened her, and she opened her eyes and sat up, positive that Banyon and the crew were on their way back to the ranch. Startled to see not Banyon or any other man, but the stallion and two mares running from the direction of the ranch, Carly quickly scooted behind the nearest tree so the horses wouldn't see her.

She glanced to her horse and saw him lift his head and look at the others, but he immediately lost interest and began grazing again. The stallion and mares showed no interest in the gelding, either, and they raced on by as if he weren't there.

Carly felt the quickened beating of her heart. This was incredibly exciting. It was also sort of funny. Banyon and his men had passed this way hours before in their search for the stallion, and while they were out looking for him, probably many miles from here by now, he, brighter than average thief, had stolen two more mares from the ranch.

"But exactly where are you taking them?" Carly whispered, getting on her knees and then on her feet to watch the trio as they galloped farther up the old riverbed. And then, very close to some large whitish boulders, they disappeared, and she blinked as though she'd been watching an apparition.

Rushing over to her horse, she untied the reins from the tree and hurriedly mounted. Riding to the boulders she realized that the ground was so hard-packed in this particular spot there were no hoof marks. The stallion must grasp that concept, she thought in amazement. He must realize that he and his ladies were leaving no trail! And Banyon and his men must have ridden right past this spot today—and how many other days—and never caught on. Oh, this was fantastic. She certainly knew something that Banyon did not, and it made her feel giggly and girlish to put one over on Banyon.

Eagerly then, she urged her horse into another forest of pine trees. Occasionally, much to her delight, she spotted an indentation in a patch of soft ground that could only have been made by a horse's hoof. She kept close track of the time, having found time to be an excellent way of keeping track of distance yesterday, and after forty minutes she could see a clearing ahead.

Something told her that she was very close to the stallion's lair, and her body pulsed with excitement. At the very edge of the trees she pulled the gelding to a halt. Before her was an emotionally moving sight. The clearing was lovely, bright with sunlight and containing lush grass and a small herd of horses. Carly's breath caught in her throat when she spotted Goldie. "Serendipity," Carly whispered. If this wasn't a fortunate, accidental discovery, she didn't know the meaning of the word.

Carly then cautiously turned the gelding's head and returned to the cover of the trees. She dismounted, tethered the horse to a branch and then tiptoed back to another tree to keep herself concealed while she studied the mares, grazing peacefully in belly-deep grass.

Even Banyon's bad humor would be appeased when she told him about this, Carly thought. She was still digesting that smugly satisfying image when the stallion's head came up suddenly, as though he was sniffing the air. *Oh, no, he knows I'm here!* Carly drew back behind the tree and waited a few minutes before taking another peek. The stallion was circling the mares, snorting and tossing his head. *He's protecting his ladies! Oh, he's magnificent. I've never seen another horse to compare.*

Her next feeling was shock; the stallion had started galloping toward her!

Instead of turning tail and running into the trees, Carly became very still. For some reason she wasn't afraid. *He won't harm me, I know he won't.*

The stallion stopped about ten feet from the forest and looked directly at her. Carly's pulse went wild, but she stood her ground and looked back. She got the strangest sensation then, as though something mystical was passing between herself and that glorious animal.

And then, as quickly as he'd galloped over, the stallion turned around, kicked up his heels and returned to his mares.

Carly released a long-held breath. Never in her life had she experienced anything close to what had just occurred. An intense elation saturated her system, and she knew in her soul that in time she could make friends with that stallion.

When she finally mounted the gelding and started back to the ranch, her mind was made up. She would not be telling Banyon one word about her discovery today. The mares were perfectly safe, and she was not going to be the instrument whereby Banyon and his men roared out to the clearing to reclaim the mares and to shoot that beautiful stallion.

Feeling high as a kite, Carly decided to eat dinner with the men that evening. Avoiding them, simply because they were men, no longer seemed sensible. Besides, it was time that she faced the fact that all men weren't mean-minded abusive wretches, as her ex had been during their marriage.

When she walked into the dining room, every eye turned

her way. She smiled brightly and said hello. Several of the
men returned her greeting, and Carly filled a plate at the long
table of food served buffet-style, then looked for an empty
chair at the many tables.

There was one that was relatively close to where Banyon
was sitting, but she ignored it and walked over to another
vacant chair between two men. They nodded and smiled, and
she smiled at them.

"Is it okay if I sit here?" she asked.

"Yes, ma'am, it sure is," one man replied. After Carly
was settled and eating, he said, "I know your pa. He's a fine
man."

"Yes, he is," Carly agreed.

Jake was keeping an eye on Carly chatting with the men
at her table, and he realized that she looked very much like
the cat that had just eaten the canary. What had happened
today to cause such a smug expression on her face? he
thought with a narrowing of his eyes. Whatever it was, he
was positive he wouldn't like it. She'd gone riding again,
Barney had told him. *She went to look for you and the men,
Jake. Didn't you see her?*

Jake hadn't been in the best of moods when he and the
crew returned to the ranch. They'd been on the trail of the
stallion and Goldie for miles, for hours, and then, in that old
riverbed, they'd lost the trail. The stallion was a sly one, that
was certain. It was as though he could think and knew that
his tracks would be lost in all of that ancient river rock.

But Jake could think, too, and now he was pretty sure that
the stallion's stronghold was somewhere in the vicinity of
that winding riverbed. The problem was that it went on for
miles and miles, far into the wilderness of the mountains,
which took in a great deal of territory. Today he and the
crew had failed, but they would pick up that devil's trail
again, eventually. Jake couldn't have the entire crew searching for that trail every day—he couldn't neglect the ranch

that much—but he could send two or three men out each morning. Sooner or later he'd get results.

A burst of laughter from Carly's table brought Jake's thoughts from the stallion and back to her. Why in hell had she gone looking for him and the crew today? To get herself lost again? he thought disgustedly. Damn, she was an irritating woman.

But she was also a beautiful woman, a sensual woman, and he relived holding and kissing her in that clearing yesterday until his body started reacting and he had to clear his mind or accept some consequences he didn't dare cause.

Resenting her for that, too, Jake finished eating. Carly's good humor annoyed Jake so much that when supper was over and she left the dining room, he got up from his table and left, too. Outside he called, "Carly!"

She stopped walking, turned around and waited for him to catch up with her. "You called?" she drawled.

Her sarcasm renewed Jake's irritation. "I need to talk to you."

Carly shrugged and started walking toward the house again. "So, talk."

Jake kept stride with her. "Where did you go today?"

She gave a snort of derisive laughter. "I hardly think that's any of your business. I'm not one of your crew members, you know."

Jake flushed. "I know damn well who you are! I wonder sometimes if you do."

They had reached the house, and Carly went in first. Jake was close behind, and he shut the door. His eyes were accusatory. "You went riding again today. Barney told me you went looking for me and the men."

"And what if I did?" She glared at him. "You're not my keeper, Banyon. I'll go riding anytime I feel like it. Don't worry," she added sweetly. "I'll stick with geldings."

"Yeah, you learned the hard way to stay away from the mares," Jake growled. "But did it ever once occur to you that I might feel responsible for your safety while you're on this ranch?''

She rolled her eyes. "That's ridiculous, but feel anything you wish. In the meantime I will do what *I* wish!''

"Including getting lost again," Jake said dourly.

"Oh, give it a rest. I am not going to get lost again. In fact, I'm learning the layout of the ranch pretty darned well." Carly couldn't completely contain the self-satisfaction she felt about her discovery today, and she realized that she would just love to tell Banyon about it and see the look on his face. While she couldn't do that, she could tell him one thing. "I easily found your tracks today and I followed you and the men to what looked to me like an old riverbed. I lost your trail there and came back to the ranch."

Jake's countenance darkened. "After what happened yesterday you went back to those foothills?"

"It was where *you* went, wasn't it? Don't bother to answer. You started your search for the stallion in the exact place you found me at yesterday. When Barney told me what you and the crew intended doing today, I knew precisely where you would start. And put this in your pipe and smoke it. I didn't have one ounce of trouble locating that spot."

"Well, explain this," Jake said angrily. "Why were you looking for us in the first damned place?"

"To stop you from shooting that stallion," Carly retorted in a strident, belligerent voice. "And if you had found him, he would be dead right now, wouldn't he? Let me tell you something, Banyon. If you dare to shoot that stallion, you'll wish you hadn't. I guarantee that I will raise so much hell you'll think the whole damn sky caved in on you."

Jake opened his mouth to tell her that he didn't now nor ever intend to shoot the stallion, but he instantly closed it again. He couldn't remember ever being more angry with anyone before. How dare Carly issue ultimatums to him? He actually relished the idea of her worrying about something that would never happen.

And so he said instead, in a deadly quiet tone of voice, "Don't you be telling me what to do on this ranch. You might be Stu's daughter, but that relationship doesn't give you any right to order me around. You're a guest here and nothing more. Try to remember that."

Carly felt a spiking burst of anger. She should remind Banyon that he was an employee, the overbearing jerk. Something stopped her from going that far, and she said, "And you might be a friend of Dad's, but that relationship doesn't give you the right to order me around! Maybe you should try to remember that!"

They hadn't turned on a light upon entering the house, and the kitchen was almost colorless from evening shadows. They stood no more than a foot apart and glared furiously at each other in the fading light. Jake thought of telling her to pack her bags and get the hell off the ranch. *You'll do things my way or else!* If she was the only person involved, he'd call for the helicopter himself and make damned sure she got on it!

But he couldn't forget Stuart in this tension-filled drama; he couldn't offend Stu. Jake's hands were tied as far as Carly Paxton was concerned, and it was a bitter pill for him to swallow.

"Well?" she said acridly, wondering if this malicious little argument was over or if Banyon still had an arsenal of orders and insults to lay on her.

That one word, put so challengingly, made Jake see red. Without thinking, he took the one step that had been like no man's land between them and grabbed her by the shoulders.

Carly yelped and tried to shake off his hands. "What do you think you're doing now?" she shrieked.

"This," he snarled, and yanked her forward. His mouth came down on hers, hard.

He was kissing her again? What was wrong with him? She did what she could to break away. She pushed on his chest and tried to kick his shins. But nothing she did fazed him, and he continued to kiss her, roughly, possessively. Carly kept fighting him, vowing silently to brain him the second she got loose. Why in heaven's name would Banyon kiss her a second time when he could just barely tolerate speaking to her?

And then she realized that her head was spinning. She got dizzier still when his mouth softened and his kiss became sensual. Something flip-flopped in the pit of her stomach, and before she knew what was happening, she was kissing him back.

Exactly like yesterday, Jake was thunderstruck by the intense desire that exploded between them. He broke the kiss to grab a breath of air, then immediately reclaimed her lips. His hands slid down her back to her hips, and he pulled her closer to the throbbing ache behind the fly of his jeans. She made a small gasping sound deep in her throat, as though objecting to such intimacy, but then she snuggled against him, at the same time permitting his tongue to slide into her mouth. Her arms went up around his neck, and her fingers twined into the hair at the back of his head.

They were plastered together so tightly, and kissing each other so frantically, that Jake knew exactly where this was heading. Right or wrong never entered the picture. Forgotten was his past, his oath to stay away from women and the fact that he'd done exactly that for almost five years, without regrets or remorse, too. But right now Jake was too aroused to think of anything but bringing this wildly passionate session to its logical conclusion.

He pulled the tail of her shirt from the waistband of her jeans and slid one hand under the shirt to unhook her bra. His next move was to bring his hand around to squeeze between their interlocked bodies to caress her the way he wanted to. He groaned at the pleasure of touching and holding her bare breasts, and felt her nipples harden against his palm.

Carly groaned, too. Their kisses had become brief, gasping

contacts, and she felt his lips on her nose, her cheeks, her eyelids. She wanted more…more. She wanted him undressed and…and…

For some reason reality returned with a bang, and when she pushed against his chest this time, he stumbled backwards.

"Carly," he whispered hoarsely, pleadingly.

She stared at him and wondered what in heaven's name had come over her? She didn't even like men anymore, and she sure as hell didn't want to sleep with one! Her legs were trembling, and she clasped the back of a chair for support.

"How dare you?" she spat, and wished her own voice wasn't so telltale hoarse. He'd gotten to her, no question about it, but she would die before admitting it, especially to him.

Still aroused to the point of pain, Jake could only think of how beautiful she looked with her hair mussed and her shirt-tail hanging out of her jeans. The soft fullness of her breasts was still on his hand, and her kisses were still on his lips. Confusion dazed his brain. Why had she cooperated with such abandonment, then put on the brakes?

And then her demeaning question finally registered, and he began to cool down. "How dare I? What about how daring you were?"

"You took advantage of me," she cried. "Again, I might add, the same way you did yesterday. What in hell's wrong with you?"

Jake thought for a moment and found that he couldn't disagree with her accusation. Even so, she wasn't entirely blameless. "All right, I should never have touched you. But let's not forget that you kissed back. Both times," he added, doing a little accusing himself.

"Oh, I fully intend to forget it," she said scornfully. Her legs were getting stronger, and she let go of the chair. "If your massive ego makes you think a few kisses mean anything to me, think again. And don't you ever touch me again, you…you Neanderthal! Maybe men grab women and force themselves upon them around here, but they don't where I come from!''

Carly knew that she was lashing out at Banyon because she had kissed back. But even knowing that her anger was far from being justified, she couldn't stop herself from expressing it. In fact, if a man ever deserved a slap in the face, it was him.

The second the idea entered her mind, she rushed forward and took a swing at him. He grabbed both of her hands so fast that she was stunned by his speed.

His looked down at her from his advantageous height with eyes that were burning like two live coals. ''I wouldn't advise you to try that again,'' he said coldly.

''Meaning you'd slap me back?'' she taunted, though a chill went up her spine. Her ex had slapped her numerous times—unquestionably the most destructive factor of their deteriorating marriage—and now she was fool enough to try and slap a man like Banyon? Good Lord.

''I've never laid a harsh hand on a woman before but I will not accept that sort of behavior from anyone, man or woman.''

Carly's stomach sank. He was right, she was wrong, and she was internally shriveling with embarrassment. She would say no more about ''slaps,'' and she certainly wouldn't try anything so foolhardy and, yes, sickening again. But she was still angry over another pass and had to say something. ''Don't think I didn't catch on right away that you didn't want me here, Banyon, because I did. You've been argumentative and…and nasty from our first conversation. You probably can't help yourself because you have no other personality. You're boring, Banyon. There are other things in the world besides this ranch, but I bet you've never thought of that, have you?''

''Don't talk so stupidly.'' Jake let go of her hands and started for the door.

"You...you total jerk, I'm not stupid!"

"Then stop acting as though you are." Jake yanked the door open and walked out.

The door slammed shut and Carly stood in the darkening kitchen with tears dribbling down her cheeks. Why had she kissed him back, why? And how did he have the power to make her so crazy?

If it weren't for that stallion and her determination to keep him alive, she would go home, Carly thought sullenly. Damn Jake Banyon, damn him to hell! He had bested her on every point this evening, and she hated him. How did he have the nerve to kiss her senseless and then call her stupid?

You are stupid. How did you have the nerve to behave like a sex-starved tart and then accuse him of taking advantage of you?

Listlessly Carly climbed the stairs to the second floor. After a shower, she crawled into bed. And since sleep was the only thing that would eradicate Jake Banyon from her mind, she prayed for blessed oblivion.

Fortunately, her body was tired enough to let go, and she was asleep in minutes. She didn't hear Jake when he returned to the house, not even when he stood outside her door and wondered if he shouldn't attempt to make amends for this evening's disaster. He almost knocked, but then he dropped his hand and stoically continued on to his own room. He and Carly Paxton would never be friends; he might as well face it.

The problem with that conclusion was that he knew now that he wanted a lot more from Carly than mere friendship. For the first time in years he wanted a woman, and not just any woman, either. He wanted his boss's daughter. Damn her, she was destroying all the peace of mind that he'd worked so hard to attain. It wasn't fair.

Six

Jake put in a bad night. Every hour or so he woke up to think about Carly in bed just down the hall. What did she sleep in? He would bet it was something silky...or maybe she slept in nothing at all. That image was so nerve shattering that Jake muttered some vile words and pounded his pillow into another shape.

Then he lay there and resented Carly for disturbing his peace, for bringing back his own past, for making him hot and horny and lustful. Strange as it was, when he'd been worried about a woman visiting the ranch and all the problems she could cause, racking desire for her body had not been one of his concerns.

Or had it? Had his subconscious known he would respond to any reasonably attractive woman after living without the opposite sex for so long? Was that how his subconscious saw Carly, as a partner for a good, lusty romp in bed?

Groaning out loud, Jake yanked the pillow over his head. How in hell was he going to survive her visit?

And was there any way he could shorten her stay without offending Stuart?

Thinking of Stuart sobered Jake further. Slowly he removed the pillow from over his head. He stared at the dark ceiling and thought of Carly's defiance. *You are not my keeper, Banyon, and I'll go where I please, when I please.* Maybe those were not her exact words, but Jake recalled her attitude precisely. Obviously she was not going to heed any warnings from him, not when she acted as though she believed he was telling her to be careful on the ranch just to prove his superiority or some damn thing.

And what if her own stupid defiance got her hurt? A chill went up Jake's spine at the thought of telling Stu that kind of news. Jake anticipated a call from his boss any day now. Stuart should be getting back from London and even if Carly wasn't at the ranch, he would phone Jake.

No, Jake decided, he could not let his boss's daughter get injured because of her own stubborn determination to do anything she pleased.

And he knew, too, just how to prevent Carly from taking any further long rides by herself, going only God knew where and risking her neck with unfamiliar horses. She wouldn't like it, but that was just plain tough.

Feeling a little better, Jake turned to his side and shut his eyes.

After waking up the next morning, Carly lay in bed for a while, just thinking. She still believed she could make friends with the stallion, but it would hardly happen overnight, and how much time did she have before someone found that clearing? If only she wasn't so ignorant in the ways of befriending a wild horse. And who could she ask for tips without arousing suspicion? Barney? One of the other men? Banyon?

Carly almost hooted out loud over considering Jake in that scenario. The truth was that Banyon would catch on quickly

if she started asking questions about making friends with a
wild horse. And she really didn't want to give him any op-
portunities to make another pass. And just being alone for a
simple conversation could do that, she thought as a warm,
tingling sensation suddenly stole her breath.

"No!" she whispered in shock. A few stolen kisses meant
nothing! She should not be feeling overheated and giddy
from just the memories.

But, damn, that man could kiss!

Carly drew a shaky breath, muttered, "Get over it," threw
back the covers and got up. Admiring a man's kissing tech-
nique could get a woman in big trouble, and she was not
going to indulge in ridiculous fantasy ever again. Real-life
relationships were not even close to the romantic fantasies
young girls dreamed about; it was a lesson she had learned
the hard way.

Still, however it had happened, she *had* learned it, and she
knew in her soul that she was not ready for another man,
even if his kisses did make her hair stand on end.

Irked because she was still thinking about Banyon on a
personal level, Carly took off her nightgown, turned on the
cold water spray in the shower and stepped into the stall.

"Yipes!" she yelled as the cold water hit her bare skin.

But it worked. Her thoughts were no longer steamy.

Carly prepared and ate breakfast in the house, all the while
planning the day ahead. If she was going to succeed in making friends with the stallion, she dare not waste any time.
She would ride out to the clearing and check his reaction to
her today. That seemed like a sensible first step, even though
she had no idea what she would do after that.

Dressed for riding and carrying a small bag of apples—
just in case a few apples might tempt the stallion into friendship—Carly went through the kitchen door and stepped out
onto the back porch.

A man jumped up from a chair, smiled and touched the brim of his hat. "Good morning, ma'am."

Carly eyed him warily. He was one of the older members of the crew, with graying hair and mustache, already a familiar figure to her, but why on earth was he sitting on the back porch instead of doing some kind of cowboy work somewhere on the ranch?

"Good morning," she said slowly. She thought of asking him point-blank what he was doing out there, but decided that she really didn't care. What the men did or did not do was Banyon's job. *Let him worry about it.* She took the stairs to the ground and began walking away, but after about four steps she realized the cowhand was right behind her.

She stopped walking and turned around. "Are you following me?"

"Yes, ma'am."

Her eyes widened incredulously. "You're following me? For God's sake, why?"

"Jake's orders, ma'am."

"No way!" she exclaimed angrily. "Where's Jake now?"

"Couldn't say, ma'am."

Carly looked around in exasperation, then glared at the cowboy. "You don't know or you won't tell me?"

"I'd tell you if I knew, ma'am. Why wouldn't I?"

"Oh, for pity's sake, stop calling me ma'am," she said irritably. "Now you listen to me. I have no idea why Jake wants you following me around, but I will not have it. Do you understand?"

"Yes, ma'am."

She waited for him to leave, but he just kept standing there. "It doesn't matter to you what I say, does it? You take your orders from Jake, and that's the long and the short of it."

"Yes, ma'am. Do you wanna know my name, ma'am?"

She almost shouted, "Why in hell would I want to know your name?" but she stifled that impulse and said instead, "Yes, of course."

"It's Deke Johnson, ma'am."

"Okay, Deke. Now, let's get to the bottom of this. When did Jake tell you to follow me?"

"This morning, ma'am. Right after breakfast."

"Carly. My name is Carly. Please, no more 'ma'ams.' Did Jake tell you why he wanted me followed? I mean, is he expecting me to dynamite a barn or something?"

Deke frowned under the wide brim of his hat. Obviously Carly's sarcasm had gone over his head. "Dynamite a barn? He never said anything about dynamite, ma'am. He just said to stay with you all day. If you go riding, I go riding. If you take a walk, I take a walk. I think he just wants to make sure you're all right."

Carly's entire system tensed with frustration. There was no way she could ride out to that clearing with Deke on her heels. Jake was going to make damn sure that she didn't get lost again, or do something—as had occurred yesterday—that he didn't learn about because she wouldn't tell him.

"I do not need a bodyguard," she snapped, then told herself to calm down. Taking her anger at Banyon out on Deke, who was only doing his assigned job for the day, was totally unjust. *But just wait till I see Banyon again!* Though seething inside, she managed a reasonably normal smile for Deke. "I'm going back to the house. See you later."

Every time Carly peeked out a back window, there was Deke. She actually saw Barney deliver lunch to him, which really fried her. Probably every man on the place was chuckling over Jake's ingenious way of keeping an eye on the boss's greenhorn daughter, and after a while she thought of the humiliation Banyon was heaping on her by giving the men on this ranch such a good reason to laugh.

It was while she was fuming and pacing, going from room to room on the first floor and planning brilliantly scathing insults to throw at Banyon when he finally returned to the house that day, that she realized her thoughts weren't *all* about him and his skulduggery; she found herself wondering again why her father had let the house get so run-down.

But, on second thought, was it actually run-down, or was it just in need of a good cleaning? Certainly soap, water and a scrub brush would eliminate a lot of the dinginess, and some good-quality polish would work miracles with the woodwork and furniture.

Carly eyed the upholstered furniture in each first-floor room—soiled but not terribly worn—and then the carpeting—also soiled but not irreparably worn.

She couldn't resist giving it a try, and she searched through cupboards in the kitchen and laundry room for cleaning supplies that might still be usable. She found an ancient vacuum cleaner that created far more dust than it picked up, but upon examination Carly discovered that all it needed was a new bag. But, of course, there wasn't one, and the cleaning agents she did manage to round up were pretty much dried up or not at all what she had in mind. This would be a major housecleaning project, and it required the best products available. Rather, she thought irritably, she would have to get by with what the stores in Tamarack carried.

"Okay, so be it," she said impatiently. "I hope you like shopping, Deke Johnson, because I'm going to town!" After dashing upstairs for her purse, she plucked the car keys from the hook in the kitchen and went out the back door. Deke got to his feet. Carly smiled sweetly. "I'm driving to Tamarack to do some shopping." Without waiting to see how he took that information, she left the back porch and headed for the garage and the car.

It was definitely her turn to chuckle, but she tactfully kept it under wraps. Obviously Jake hadn't suggested to Deke that his charge might decide to get in the car and leave the ranch, and poor Deke wasn't sure what he should do about it. Apparently he decided he'd better go shopping, too, because Carly could hear him running behind her to catch up.

Laughing under her breath, she entered the garage through

its side door. Inside, she began looking around for a switch
or button that would raise the heavy wood door so the car
could exit, then realized there was no overhead gadgetry and
the large front door had to be opened by hand.

Deke looked in through the side door. "Are we going to
Tamarack, ma'am?"

"Carly," she said with a look of annoyance over another
"ma'am." "I'm going to Tamarack. Guess it's up to you
where you're going, if you're leaving at all, that is." Marching around the car to the big door, she located a handle near
the floor, bent over to take hold of it, then straightened up
and brought the door up with her. It felt like it weighed a
ton, and she said disgustedly, "Good grief, I would think
someone would modernize this place. At the very least Banyon could hire a person to clean the house once in a while."

"Uh, yes, ma'am," Deke replied, sounding pretty confused about this whole turn of events.

Carly climbed behind the wheel of the car, then rolled
down the window. "If you're coming along so you can obey
Banyon's moronic orders, you'd better get in." She laughed
right out loud when Deke practically ran to the passenger's
side of the car.

"And buckle your seat belt," she told him even before he
was fully settled. "Sometimes I get to thinking about something else and drive a little too fast. I wouldn't want you
getting hurt." Carly enjoyed the wary glance Deke sent her.
She rarely drove faster than the speed limit, but she couldn't
resist hassling Deke some, even if he was just an innocent
pawn of Jake Banyon's.

Starting the engine, she revved it a few times, then put the
shifting lever in reverse and shot out of the garage like a
bullet. Slamming on the brakes, she jumped out and hurried
to shut the big door. Returning to the car she latched her own
seat belt with a sugary smile at Deke, then said brightly,
"And we're off! Hang on to your hat, Deke."

Much too her amusement, he did it.

Jake just happened to be walking from one barn to another when he heard the car start and then back out of the garage with the speed of a cannonball. Scowling, he changed directions and headed for the car. He broke into a jog when Carly got out and shut the garage door, but then she immediately got back into the car and Jake was still too far away to do more than yell her name. If she heard him, she didn't let on, and in the next second she, the car and Deke Johnson were gone, speeding down the driveway toward the road.

"At least Deke's with her," Jake muttered. "So she won't get into too much trouble."

It occurred to him then that for a woman who was reportedly despondent over a bad marriage and divorce, Carly could sure keep everyone around her on their toes. If she was down in the dumps, it didn't show. Either she was damned good at concealing her feelings or Stu was overly protective of his only child and worried for nothing.

Watching the car kick up dust until it was out of sight, Jake felt a most peculiar longing: He wished it were him going off with Carly, instead of Deke.

Grunting in sour-faced disapproval of just about the dumbest wish to ever weaken a man's knees, he turned around and began walking like a man with a purpose.

"So tell me, Deke, how long have you worked at the ranch?" Carly was driving sensibly on the highway, having had her fun with Deke while still on ranch property.

"'Bout ten years."

"Longer than Banyon," Carly murmured. "Do you know him very well?"

"Nope. No one does. Jake keeps to himself."

Carly glanced Deke's way. "Are you saying that none of the men know anything about him? Where did he come from? What did he do before going to work for my father? Was he ever married?"

"I don't like to gossip, ma'am."

"Carly," she said sternly. "Deke, if you don't start calling me Carly, I'm going to call you sir."

Deke laughed. "That'd be pretty funny."

"Say my name," she commanded.

"Well, heck, ma'am, you're Stu Paxton's daughter."

"So what? I still have a name, and I want you to use it."

Deke sighed. "Okay, if you say so."

"I do say so. Now, tell me what you know about Banyon." She sent him a quick, reassuring smile. "Exchanging information isn't gossiping, Deke."

"Since when?" he asked dryly.

Carly couldn't help laughing. But she still intended to hear anything Deke might know about Jake and she didn't question her curiosity, either. Why wouldn't she be curious about a gruff, surly, good-looking guy who had practically turned her inside out with a few kisses? She'd come to the ranch positive that it would be a long time before she felt anything but disdain for any man, and in a very few days Banyon had gotten under her skin.

When her laughter died, Carly said again, "So, what do you know about Banyon?"

"Well, let's see," Deke said thoughtfully, almost lazily. "I guess Jake doesn't like people very much, 'cause I've never seen any sign of him having friends. Leastwise, none have come to the ranch that I heard about."

Carly diligently watched the road ahead, though her mind was more on Banyon being friendless than on her driving. Did *friendless* also mean he had no girlfriends? For some unfathomable reason that picture cheered her more than anything else had in quite a long while.

In the next instant, though, her thoughts drifted to the stallion again. Cleaning a house was a good project for a woman with time on her hands. Then, too, bantering with and teasing Deke Johnson was kind of fun. But eventually someone was going to find that clearing, and with Deke shadowing her every move there wasn't a darned thing she could do to stop the horrible end Banyon planned to bring to that beautiful animal.

"Deke," she said calmly, "did Banyon indicate that you or one of the other men would be following me around from here on in?"

"Nope. Just told me to stick with you today, ma'am."

"I see," Carly murmured, though, in truth, the only thing she really saw was red. Banyon was going to get one extremely furious piece of her mind at the very first opportunity, and she hoped, ardently, that opportunity would knock before night fell this day. How dare he decide she needed a bodyguard, or that *he* needed a spy!

With the stallion uppermost in her mind again, Carly asked, "Deke, have you seen that fabulous black stallion?"

"The wild one?"

"Yes, the wild one. Have you seen him?"

"Nope, can't say that I have."

"And yet you would shoot him if Banyon told you to?"

Deke turned his head and gave her a startled look. "You sure do ask hard questions, ma'am. Sorry," he added when Carly sent him a disgusted glance. "I meant to say your name."

"No question is hard if you have an answer, Deke. Would you shoot that stallion if Banyon told you to?"

Deke thought a moment, then said, "Jake wouldn't tell anyone to shoot an animal without a darned good reason. So yes, if he told me to do it, I would."

"That's abominable! You should feel totally ashamed of yourself!"

Carly's outburst made Deke cringe. It was obvious, even to Carly, that he hadn't expected it and that she'd scared the tar out of him. Good, she thought angrily, and clamped her lips tightly together with the intention of not saying another word to him today or any other. Men! Vile, disgusting, violent creatures, every one of them.

* * *

When they got back to the ranch, Deke helped Carly carry her purchases into the house. Then he went outside and sat on the porch again.

Carly gave a resentful sigh and began unloading sacks. It would soon be time for dinner, and Deke would undoubtedly go and eat with the other men. Carly would finally be freed of his watchful eyes, but the day was pretty much shot. Certainly she couldn't go out to that clearing with nightfall only a few hours away. Also, it was really too late in the day to start any serious housecleaning.

Her thoughts suddenly changed directions: What had Banyon done today? If he or any of the men had found the stallion and harmed him...?

The frustration and resentment that Carly had kept fairly well controlled all day began boiling over, and she slammed cupboard doors as she put things away. She used a few cuss words, too, and when one door didn't stay closed on the first try, she gave it several hard slams.

When everything she'd bought was out of sight, she plopped down on a chair at the kitchen table to fume and fuss and worry. Anger was a big part of her mood—anger that Banyon had outwitted her so easily today. He didn't want her going out riding alone and he'd found a way to stop her. Of course, if she didn't have something to hide, she probably wouldn't care if someone rode with her.

Damn him! Fury nearly choked Carly, and she thought of the pleasure that throttling Banyon would give her.

Better yet, if there was just some way to outwit *him!*

Carly narrowed her eyes, thinking that, yes, of course, she had to play *his* game. Today he'd gotten and held the upper hand; tomorrow would be her turn.

And it would be so easy, she thought with a smug smile, as a simple but effective plan took shape in her brain. Why, she wasn't even angry anymore!

But she must appear to be when Banyon comes in for his before-dinner shower, or he might get suspicious.

It was about twenty minutes later that Carly heard men's voices and knew that Jake had arrived and was talking to Deke before he came in. She deliberately went to the window over the sink so Banyon could see her, and she put on the most furious expression she could manage, glaring daggers at him.

It delighted her that he blinked a couple of times when he saw her, as though startled, so she continued to stare and glare and was again rewarded with a show of nervousness. Banyon shifted his weight from one foot to the other and turned his back to her, definite signs, she decided, that she was making him uncomfortable.

"Good," she whispered. Apparently he was expecting her to be angry, and why on earth would she disappoint him?

Deke finally left the porch and walked off, and Jake started toward the kitchen door. Carly hurriedly moved away from the window, leaned her hips against a counter and belligerently folded her arms across her chest.

Jake walked in and stopped. He'd never seen a more clearly defined portrayal of outrage than what Carly was projecting and he wondered if maybe he'd gone just a tad too far today.

Carly spoke with fire in her eyes. "You are, without a doubt, the worst case of stunted development I have ever had the misfortune of running into. How dare you destroy my day with a baby-sitter?"

"A what?" Jake frowned.

"Do you think I'm some idiot child that needs constant supervision? If anyone on this ranch needs a baby-sitter, Banyon, it's you, not me. Have Deke follow you around for a day and see how you like it. I swear to God that if I see his face tomorrow morning, I will scream so loudly they'll hear me in Tamarack." Carly raised her chin. "They might even hear me in London."

Jake had been taking her tirade as justifiable until that final threat. Then his own hackles rose, and he advanced on her with fire in his eyes. Throwing off his hat, he grabbed her by the upper arms and glared right into her face.

"Making trouble between me and Stuart would be the easiest thing in the world for you to do," he growled. "But I wouldn't advise it, particularly since I was only thinking of your safety when I told Deke to stay with you today."

Something happened then. Carly said nothing, Jake said no more. They merely stood there looking at each other. Volatile emotions, unexpressed verbally but feeling thick enough to slice, passed between them.

Carly felt as though she were sinking into the depths of the bluest eyes she'd ever seen, which she feared was as dangerous as falling into shark-infested waters. But she couldn't seem to save herself, she kept sinking deeper. Her lips were strangely dry, and she moistened them with the tip of her tongue, which Jake watched as though hypnotized by the sight.

Carly finally found her voice, although it came out of her mouth as more of a hoarse, strangled croak. "Wha...what are we doing?"

"I think we're both fighting against nature." Jake, too, sounded hoarse. "And maybe I'm losing my battle." Groaning, he pressed himself closer to her and whispered into her hair, "I can't seem to keep my hands off you. Did you cast a spell on me when you stepped off the helicopter? That was when this agony started, the second I saw you."

Her hips were against the counter, and Jake was against her. She could feel every manly contour of his body, and she was suddenly flushed and in a fever of longing and physical dissatisfaction such as she'd never before experienced. She knew what he wanted and she knew what she wanted, and it was such a surprise that she wanted to make love that it didn't occur to her to stop this before it got out of hand.

She began moving against him, seeking what her body was aching for, and he responded in haste, unzipping her jeans and pushing them down her hips and legs, along with her panties. Then he lifted her to sit on the counter, and he quickly got rid of her shoes so he could also get rid of her jeans and panties.

It was then a simple matter to spread her thighs and place himself between them. It was at that moment that he began kissing her, and in the throes of the wildest passion of her life, Carly felt him pull her to the very edge of the counter and complete their union.

She moaned and tore her mouth from his, as she wasn't getting enough air through her nose. Her heart was beating so hard, and the thrills were compounding so fast that she realized a profound fact of her life: She had never felt so much with a man as she did with Banyon. She had never gone up in flames—or was it down in flames—as she was now with him moving in and out of her and kissing her throat and then, after opening her shirt and undoing her bra, her breasts. She heard his hard breathing, and her own, and her mind swam dizzily as she wrapped her legs around him and twined her fingers into his hair.

And then, as quickly as it had started, it was over. They cried out together, and the final pleasure was so intense for Carly that she was afraid of blacking out. Laying her head on his chest, she sucked in huge breaths of air and waited for her system to calm down.

Jake's first sensible thought was that she was Stu's daughter. *My God, where was my brain?*

He pulled away from her so fast that she nearly toppled over. She had to catch and steady herself because he was scrambling to pull up his underwear and jeans, and the look on his face struck her as pure horror. He could not have put on a more insulting expression, and she knew at that second that it might have been incredible for her but it had only been mundane, at best, for him.

Wounded to the quick, she jumped down from the counter, grabbed her things from the floor and ran from the kitchen.

She honestly felt as though her heart was bleeding.

Seven

Refreshed and fully dressed again, Carly sat on the bed in her room, trembled like a leaf in the wind and asked herself why she felt so devastated. It wasn't as though this was her first emotional blow from a man, after all. What she'd gone through during her marriage would fill a book.

Regardless, she felt shattered in a brand-new way. Was it because making love with Banyon had been so soul stirring, almost wickedly incredible? She'd heard of sexual perfection for two people but she certainly hadn't experienced it for herself until today. Actually, she had never been what one might call a sexpot and, in fact, had years ago accepted a low sex drive as normal for her. Her ex had taunted her with words like *frigid* and *passionless,* and she'd had no defense against such malicious accusations, because with him they were more true than not.

For the first time ever Carly realized that she was as sensual as any woman. Obviously she hadn't run into the right man before. Frowning over that idea, Carly wondered how on earth Jake Banyon could be the right man. What had he done differently than the few other men that she'd slept with?

More painful to contemplate, however, was how it could have been so great for her and not for him. She would never, not for the rest of her days, forget today.

Groaning, she covered her face with her hands. They had made love without protection, but that was only a dull concern in the back of her mind. She was terribly afraid that she'd given a little too much to a man who didn't want it. Not just her body, for heaven's sake, but her heart, her soul, her mind. And she'd vowed so ardently not to do that again, and had been so positive it would be an easy oath to keep.

But that had been before meeting Jake Banyon. The man had a fatal charm, a magnetic sexuality she obviously had never been exposed to before. And he'd looked at her after it was over as though she was dirt under his feet!

Panic rose in Carly's throat, nearly choking her. She should get the hell away from here. She should pack her things, take the car and drive to…to…well, almost anywhere would do, just so she wouldn't have to face Banyon again.

But then, without warning, Carly's mood changed. If anyone should leave the Paxton ranch, it should be Banyon, not her! Carly got up to pace and think that idea through.

A few minutes later she'd made several decisions. She was not going anywhere, nor would she even hint to Banyon that he should. In fact, he was never going to know how badly he'd hurt her today. She was going to stay at the ranch and find a way to protect that stallion, and she was going to do it right under Jake Banyon's nose. And just let him try something personal with her again, the cad, just let him try. She would put him in his place so fast his head would spin.

Listening then, Carly thought she could hear the shower running in Jake's bathroom. Drawing a deep breath, she went to a mirror to check her hair and makeup, then with a granitelike determination, she walked from her bedroom and down the stairs. Going to the living room, she sat on the old

swivel stool at the piano and began playing a Beethoven so-
nata.

Jake, wearing clean clothes and with his hair still wet from
the shower, left his room and stopped in the hall when he
heard the piano. Carly wasn't a great pianist—she occasionally hit a wrong note—but her playing had passion and emo-
tion, and it touched him. Dammit, *she* touched him! She
wasn't just any woman, she meant something to him!

A great weakness washed over Jake, and he leaned against
a wall to overcome it. Was he falling for Carly? If he was it
was the shock of the century. But hadn't the die been cast in
the kitchen just a short time ago? As for offending his boss,
Jake had always viewed Stuart Paxton as a reasonable man.
It was possible that Stuart just might give his blessings to a
relationship between his daughter and ranch manager.

Jake groaned under his breath. He was rationalizing because he already wanted Carly again. Just thinking of their
wild coupling in the kitchen made him ready for more of the
same. He had to pull himself together and see things as they
really were, dammit, not the way he wished they were. The
only thing he had to offer Carly Paxton was his job, and he
worked for her dad, for hell's sake. Oh, yeah, he thought
wryly, there was his savings account in the Tamarack bank,
not because he was thrifty and practical but because he rarely
went anywhere to spend his pay.

No, he had nothing to give a woman who had lived her
entire life with everything money could buy. Accepting that
conclusion as final, Jake pushed away from the wall and went
downstairs. He went directly to the living room, because he
wanted to clear the air with Carly.

She sensed him behind her and stopped playing, leaving
her hands rest on the keys.

"Carly?"

"What?" She didn't turn around.

"Are you all right?"

She did turn then, swiveling the stool so she could see him. "Of course I'm all right. Why wouldn't I be?"

"Uh, because, well...uh, because of what happened between us," Jake stammered. Her eyes looked so intense, so beautiful in the waning, dusky light of early evening, and he wished again that circumstances were different. He could have made more of himself than he had, but then, if he hadn't gone to work for Stuart he never would have met Carly. The convolutions of his mind were almost painful. Nothing was either all black or all white, was it? And it was those gray areas, those impenetrable gray areas that confused a man so.

"Are you thinking I should be upset because of the incident in the kitchen?" Carly asked coolly. "Or maybe not upset, but something? In your mind, what should I be feeling, Jake, and why would you be concerned enough to bring it up? Surely you didn't suddenly develop a conscience, did you? Perhaps in the shower?"

Jake flushed crimson. "Uh, you know exactly what I'm getting at, don't you? What happened shouldn't have happened. You feel the same about that. It's sort of embarrassing—maybe for you, too—but..."

"Hold on, sport." Carly held up a hand, halting his humiliating assumptions. What on earth was wrong with him? Well, if she accomplished nothing else with this ridiculous discussion, she was going to do her best to head him in a different direction. "In the first place, I feel no embarrassment at all over making love with you," she said tartly. "If you're embarrassed, I'd rather not hear about it."

Jake stood there with his mouth hanging open. "Uh, guess I got the wrong idea...for...for some reason."

"Guess you did," she snapped.

"It isn't that I'm so, uh, embarrassed. I guess the, uh, bottom line is that I'd rather Stuart not, uh, hear about it."

Carly realized that she was enjoying making him squirm. "Are you going to tell him?"

For a second Jake looked confused. Then he scowled and said, "Hell, no! I was worried about you telling him."

She smirked. "Oh, get real, Banyon. I think the last father-daughter chat that Dad and I had about sex was when I went away to college. A lot of water has passed under that bridge since then, and I'm sure now that he's no more interested in my sex life than I am in his. So go and eat your dinner and forget the whole thing. To tell you the truth, I've already relegated it to my past-indiscretions trash bin, and if I can forget it so easily, I'm sure you can."

Jake felt as though someone or something had just cut off his air supply. Shock ripped through his system, feeling like jagged shards of glass. She had already forgotten it? She'd relegated it to her past-indiscretions trash bin? What in hell kind of woman was she? Did she do it with any guy who came along? If *she* was in the mood, that is?

"Yeah, I can forget it," he said with a dark scowl. "No problem there."

"I was, uh, sure there wouldn't be." *Do you have to be the most incredibly sexy, handsome guy I've ever met? Damn you, why don't you just go? Get out of here and leave me alone!*

"You might as well come with me," Jake said evenly, although sounding as though everything was just great wasn't easy to do. "You have to eat, too."

"No, thanks. I'm not very hungry, and there's a can of soup in the kitchen with my name on it. It's really all I want for...dinner. You go on. Barney and the men are probably wondering what's keeping you, and we...we wouldn't want them getting the wrong idea."

"All right. See you later." Half sick to his stomach, Jake walked out.

Half sick to *her* stomach, Carly sat on the piano stool for a long time and tried to make some sense out of the last hour. In the end she could find nothing sensible about one second of it, and she finally sighed, got up and went to the kitchen to scare up some dinner for herself.

Obviously she was still the worst judge of the opposite sex that had ever come down the pike. Obviously her destiny was to repeatedly fall for the wrong man and to trap herself in relationships that couldn't possibly do anything but cause her misery.

But in Banyon's case, did she really have to worry? The only thing worrying him, the wretch, was how her father would react to hearing about his ranch manager nailing his little girl.

Well, she hadn't been a "little" girl in a long time, not in her eyes or in her father's, and she'd been absolutely wild for Banyon's brand of lovemaking. What's more, she had no trouble admitting it.

Wouldn't it be a hoot if she got him to do it again, in spite of all his objections and red-faced embarrassment?

She laughed a little, then felt tears in her eyes. Banyon had her going in circles, no doubt about it.

Jake walked around for about an hour after supper, hoping that by the time he went back to the house, Carly would be in her room. During his meandering stroll one thought overcame dozens of others and caused him great distress: he truly felt as though some irredeemable tragedy had occurred this day, and he had caused it. Damn, if he had to develop a libido again, why not with some stranger? Why were all of his libidinous thoughts and urges aimed directly at Carly Paxton?

And dare he believe that she wouldn't tell Stuart about it? *By the way, Dad, Jake Banyon is a disgustingly lecherous and probably untrustworthy jerk. If he was as trustworthy as you've been thinking he is, would he have seduced me in the kitchen and with most of our clothes on? He was in one big hurry, I can tell you, and I guess I got swept up in the moment. But it was all his doing, Dad, and you should never trust him again.*

Jake heard that conversation in his head over and over again—with variations, of course—but always with Carly blaming him. And why wouldn't she blame him? She certainly wouldn't tell her dad that she'd seduced him, for God's sake, which wouldn't be true if she did say it.

But had he really seduced her? Hadn't she been as willing a participant as any woman he'd ever known? Had he once heard the word *no,* or any other sign of protest from her? No way. She'd been hot and hungry, and he could still feel her tongue in his mouth and her legs locked around him and drawing him deeper and deeper into the pleasures of her body.

Jake hated that he couldn't stop thinking about it, but behind every other thought was that single searing memory, and once more he found himself wishing things were different, that he could go into the house, up the stairs to Carly's room and crawl into bed with her.

Fury that his life had come full circle, and that he was once again suffering over a woman, was almost more than he could bear. Finally, he gave up on his attempts at subtlety and tact, and he went to the back door of the house and walked in.

He took only a few steps when he heard Carly's voice, coming from the office, it seemed. His heart sank then, because it was obvious that she was talking to Stuart.

"I'm serious, Dad. Why did you let me get away with not coming to the ranch when I was a kid? It's a beautiful place, and I see now that I missed an awful lot."

Jake went to the open doorway and leaned against the woodwork. Carly, who was sitting at the desk, looked up. "Jake just came in. I think you and I have covered everything so I'll give him the phone now. Bye, Dad. Call again when you can." She held out the phone, but because she didn't get up from the desk chair, Jake was on a rather short leash.

He perched on the edge of the desk and brought the phone to his ear. "Stu, when did you get back?"

"About an hour ago, Jake. Carly sounds happy. Let me thank you for that."

"Uh, I'm not sure it's my doing."

"Well, I'm sure you have something to do with it. I'm sorry I didn't call from London, but between the time difference and a hectic schedule, I simply couldn't get it done."

"No problem, Stu."

"So, how're things going? Have you caught that stallion yet?"

"Wish I could say yes, but he's a slippery devil."

Carly knew she was in the way and that she should get up and let Jake have the chair, but with him where he was and her sitting where she was, she could smell his aftershave, feel his aura, his warmth, and she could look at him, study him from head to toe, remember his kisses and how he felt inside her.

A tide of heat began in the pit of her stomach and radiated outwardly from there. She wanted him…oh, how she wanted him! Her desire was so overwhelming that crazy ideas flashed through her mind, such as her reaching out to his fly and unzipping his jeans. Or she could get up and straddle his lap. She'd been getting ready for bed when the phone rang, so she was wearing a robe and nothing else. If she straddled his lap, would he get hard immediately, or would he be turned off by such brash behavior and push her away?

Her desire sort of deflated at that image. She wanted no more disdain from Jake, such as she'd seen on his face while he'd been scrambling into his clothes after their encounter in the kitchen. Carly frowned as she tried to recapture his expression in minute detail. It wasn't nearly as clear in her mind as it had been, and she was no longer positive it had been disdain. Or disgust. Or disappointment.

Dammit, what *had* it been?

She caught on then that Jake and her dad were discussing the stallion, and her lips thinned noticeably. If Banyon said one word about killing that horse, she was going to grab the phone from his hand and tell her father *her* point of view on that abominable matter, and she would not go easy on Jake, either.

"I think we have a pretty good idea of the general vicinity of his hideout, Stu. But it's not a small area, and so far we haven't found the exact location. We will, though. I'm sure it's just a matter of time."

"Has he taken any more mares?"

"Not for a couple of nights now. In fact, no one's spotted him for several days."

"Maybe he took his ladies and left the area," Stuart speculated.

"Could be, but it's really too soon to celebrate that possibility. Don't worry, we'll get him." Jake glanced at Carly when he said that to gauge her reaction to it, and he noticed that the left lapel of her robe had gapped enough to permit a glimpse of her breast. He couldn't stop staring at that soft, lovely curve of her body, and he had to moisten his lips before talking again.

Carly looked down to see what he was staring so intently at, then raised her eyes without closing the gap. *Let him look...and want...and remember.*

Jake finally said "Good night," and put down the phone. "Your robe is open," he said gruffly to Carly.

"So?" Every feature of her face was a challenge.

And then he said something that stunned her. "Don't do this to me," he said in an agonized whisper. "Don't tempt me, Carly. I can't touch you again." Getting off the desk, he hurried from the room.

She stared after him with wide, startled eyes. Then, rising slowly, she adjusted her robe and tightened the sash. Banyon was one very strange duck, and maybe she shouldn't be fooling around with a man of his unreadable nature.

Still, she couldn't deny that "tempting" Jake Banyon was thrilling, almost beyond words.

What, for example, would he do if she walked into his

room, dropped her robe completely and climbed into bed stark naked with him?

He'd do it again, you idiot! He'd make love to you, just because you were handy, then he'd insult you with some kind of pathetic, remorseful look. Good grief, why do you do these things to yourself? How much heartache do you want, or can you take, in one lifetime?

Disgusted with herself, Carly turned off the downstairs lights and went up to her room.

Jake lay awake a long time, carrying on a debate with himself that could easily and appropriately be entitled "The Pros and Cons of a Personal Relationship with Your Boss's Daughter."

No matter how many pros he came up with, though, one con seemed to stand out as though highlighted in neon: personal relationships were damnably unpredictable things, and even if he and Carly got serious and Stuart was pleased about it, something could go wrong at the last minute and ruin everything. Who knew better than he that a woman could change her mind about a man five minutes before the nuptials?

And that would be the end of his job and the way of life he'd worked so hard to attain here at Wild Horse Ranch.

If it was cowardly of him not to want to take that risk, then he was a sniveling coward, Jake thought with no small amount of bitterness. Punching his pillow, he forced his thoughts to better days, to those tranquil weeks, months and years before Carly Paxton had gotten off that helicopter.

Would life ever be the same again? Would he ever find that wonderful tranquillity again? Would he be able to sit peacefully on the porch on summer nights, listen to and absorb the quiet and think of work schedules and ranch projects instead of Carly's body?

Cursing violently, Jake threw back the covers, got off the bed and went to a window, where he looked out at the yard lights and what could be seen of the buildings. A massive melancholy suddenly overcame him, and he felt tears sting his eyes.

How could he have been such a fool as to open this particular can of worms? Damn!

The alarm clock buzzed on Carly's nightstand, and she quickly pushed the Stop button. It was 3:00 a.m., at least an hour before Jake usually got up, and her plan would fall apart if he awoke and came charging out of his room to ask her why she was wandering around at this hour.

She had laid out her clothes last night, and she got dressed in the dark, making as little noise as possible. Leaving her bed unmade, she tiptoed from her room and silently pulled the door closed. Taking one stealthy step at a time, she made it down the stairs without a sound. Locating the flashlight she'd left with the other things she intended to take with her, she finally stepped outside onto the back porch ready to go.

It was her turn to put one over on Jake, and she couldn't help smiling about it; so far her plan had worked smooth as silk. Eyeing the yard lights, wavering slightly from a night breeze, she then glanced over to the bunkhouse. No lights there. Jake was still sleeping, and so was his crew. Barney would probably be stirring soon, so she had to move fast if she was going to get away from the compound without anyone seeing her.

Today Deke Johnson, or anyone else Jake decided to put on her heels, could go fly a kite. Jake, himself, could go fly a kite. She was going to visit that special little clearing and watch the stallion and mares, and no one would have the slightest idea where she'd gone. And wouldn't it be incredible if the stallion approached her again, as he'd done that first day? She was prepared this time, with apples and carrots in her knapsack, along with a big lunch and a canteen of water for herself.

Oh, yes, she was going to have a marvelous day.

But first she had to coax a horse to the fence around the horse pasture, then saddle him and ride away before the ranch came to life. And it was darker than pitch away from the yard lights.

Squinting wasn't working very well. Carly finally had to use the flashlight to see where she was going.

It was then that she realized how eerie it was out there at night.

No! She was not going to get all female and foolish, just because it was dark and the animals—or something—made strange noises. Why, anyone familiar with a ranch could probably identify every single sound she was hearing.

I'm going to do this, dammit, I am!

Approaching the fence around the horse pasture, she held the flashlight in one hand and an apple in the other. Then she called softly, "Here, horsie, come horsie," which sounded completely inane, even to her own ears.

And you thought you did your homework, she thought with a disdainful sniff. She could at least have found out the name of the gray gelding she'd ridden the other day.

Jake awoke with a start, then lay there and listened. Something was wrong, some off-key sound or movement. Then it hit him. The stallion! That damn thief was probably near the mare's barn and corral right now, trying to coax another one to join his harem.

Jake bounded out of bed and got dressed with the speed of light. Running from his room, he took the stairs down to the first floor two and three at a time. He hit the kitchen door still running and didn't stop running until he entered the barn where he kept the mares that were in season.

Nothing was in there that shouldn't be, and frowning, Jake went out to the corral, where three mares looked at him curiously.

But there was no sign of the stallion or of any agitation among the mares indicating the stallion might be nearby.

Jake was in the process of telling himself that he'd merely been dreaming up some trouble where there was none when he heard the sound of galloping hooves. It was coming from the geldings' pasture. He ran as fast as he could from the corral, around the barns and out to that field.

Some of the horses were milling around, as though disturbed. But disturbed by what? No stallion was interested in geldings. Still, one might cross any pasture to get where he wanted to go. Narrowing his eyes, Jake tried to see across the large field. It was too dark to see much of anything, and after a few minutes he gave up.

Walking back to the house, he tried to make sense of the last ten or fifteen minutes. There had definitely been a galloping horse, that was the only thing he was sure of. The rest of it—what had brought him awake with a sense of urgency, for instance—would probably forever remain a mystery.

Hell, there is nothing mysterious about it, he thought then with a snort of frustration. With that stallion on the loose and constantly looking for fresh mares, why would anyone with a lick of common sense question night noises?

Eight

Carly was back at the compound a few minutes before ten that morning. She was sick at heart. The stallion and mares had not been at the clearing. Signs of them were everywhere in that pretty place, but they had moved on. What really bothered Carly was her role in losing track of those valuable mares again. If she had told Jake about the clearing, the mares would have been recovered. And she could have used a little blackmail with Jake to get him to promise not to harm the stallion. *I'll tell you where he and the mares are if you swear not to kill him.*

Yes, she could have done much better than she had. Wearily dragging her heels, she walked into the house and set down her knapsack, flashlight and canteen on the kitchen table. She was just starting to make a pot of coffee when Jake walked in.

She yelped and he yelped, and she said, "Good Lord, make a noise or something. Don't sneak up on me like that. I thought you were outside somewhere."

"Yeah, well, I thought you were sleeping in. Where've you been?"

"Not that it's any of your business, but I took a ride." She finished preparing the pot and switched it on.

"Well, you must've left damned early to be back already." He remembered being jarred awake before four that morning. As understanding hit him, so did astonishment. "It was you I heard this morning!"

She looked him straight in the eye. "I left early so I didn't have to put up with Deke or somebody else shadowing me the whole darned day, as though I were a criminal or something."

"Don't be so melodramatic. You know very well why I had Deke keeping an eye on you yesterday."

Carly smiled sweetly. "To save me from myself?"

"Carly, dammit, if something happened to you while you're here, how would I explain it to your dad?"

"Oh, for crying out loud, is what Dad might do or feel about something all you think about? Your song of woe is wearing very thin, Banyon. Why don't you do both of us a favor and write a new one?"

"I happen to respect Stuart Paxton," Jake said icily, "and he respects me. Now, that might not mean anything to you, but it means a hell of a lot to me."

"Which, of course, is the reason you seduced his daughter within days of meeting her."

Jake's face turned crimson, and Carly groaned inwardly. Why on earth did she sometimes speak without thinking? "I'm sorry," she said quickly. "It was no more your fault than mine."

Jake wasn't buying her attitude, which, granted, was generous even if it wasn't remotely true. But he didn't appreciate her attempt to share the blame, when he'd caused the entire incident. She sure wouldn't have started things by kissing him!

"I know what I did was way out of line," he said curtly. "Believe me, it won't happen again."

That declaration or promise or whatever it was didn't thrill Carly in the least. She watched Jake walk out of the kitchen and realized vaguely that he must be working in the office this morning. Emotionally deflated by his intense regret, she took off her hat and jacket, piled them on top of her other things on the table and then plopped onto a chair to watch the coffee perk.

Maybe what Jake said wasn't a promise. Maybe it was a challenge. Maybe she should decipher his words as, "I can't make another pass at you, but if you're so inclined, I wouldn't say no."

"You imbecile," she muttered, aiming her name-calling at herself. The man was sorry he'd slipped. He regretted their lovemaking with every fiber of his being, and he was not apt to be sending her secret messages in perfectly simple, straightforward sentences.

Believe me, it won't happen again.

Recalling Banyon's determination while the coffee perked gradually altered Carly's mood. It wasn't going to happen again? Bet she could make it happen again. Just thinking about their first time together made her feel warm and achy, and it amazed her that she, a woman who had never enjoyed sex very much, would be sitting on that chair and plotting the seduction of a man who'd just told her—and not for the first time—that nothing personal or intimate was ever going to occur between them again.

"Oh, yeah?" she whispered as a frisson of thrill-charged excitement raced up and down her spine. Jumping up, she gathered her armload of things from the table and raced from the kitchen and up the stairs to her room. Shedding her clothes—all of them, every stitch—she grabbed her prettiest robe and her cosmetic case and ran for the bathroom, where she took a very fast shower.

In ten minutes, wearing the robe and smelling wonderfully

delicious, she returned to the kitchen, poured two cups of coffee and carried them to the office. Jake, seated at the desk, looked up in surprise.

"I thought you might like a cup of coffee," Carly purred and leaned across the desk to place one hand near his right hand, knowing full well that the loosely tied robe would gap and give him a good look at her bosom.

"Uh, thanks," Jake stammered. His eyes had darkened perceptibly because of the scenic view she'd just given him, but he knew almost at once what she was up to and he couldn't let her get away with it. She was radiantly beautiful and so sexy he was already suffering, but he had to put a stop to this. She didn't understand that he was fighting for his very life here; it was probably all fun and games for her. Well, he'd be tactful, if possible, but this was the end of the line.

When he spoke again, he wasn't stammering a bit. "I see you brought coffee for yourself, so have a seat."

"Thanks." Carly moved a chair from the front of the desk to its side, then sat and crossed her legs. Of course, her right leg protruded from the robe, and Jake had an unobstructed view of it, just as she'd planned.

"What are you working on?" Carly asked in the most innocent voice she could manage.

Jake took a sip of coffee, then cleared his throat. That robe and the way she wore it would drive any man crazy. "Just some paperwork," he said as casually as he could manage. "The usual stuff."

"The 'usual,' meaning paying bills?"

"Yeah, that's pretty usual." He'd seen her breasts, so she wasn't wearing a bra. Was she even wearing panties? The thought of her being completely naked under that flimsy robe was so provocative that Jake knew he was going to lose this skirmish if he didn't get her out of the office, and fast.

"Why are you wearing a robe?" he asked. "You were fully dressed in the kitchen a little while ago."

"I took a shower and grabbed this old thing to have my first cup of coffee of the day. That was when I thought you might enjoy one."

"I see. You didn't think of bringing me coffee till *after* you'd gotten out of the shower and put on that robe without the benefit of underwear." He looked at her across the desk with hard eyes. "You're lying, Carly. You put that robe on to deliberately inflame my thoughts."

"Really," she said coolly.

"Yes, really. And you leaned across the desk so I would see your breasts. Now you're sitting with one beautiful leg exposed, and don't try to convince me that's accidental. Would you mind if I said what I'm thinking?"

"Not at all," Carly murmured seductively.

"Okay, here it is. If you untied that sash, opened that robe, then spread your legs apart on that chair, I'd see everything you got, lady. It feels right to me, what do you think about it?"

Carly's mouth dropped open. "You...you're not serious."

"Try me. If you show me yours, I'll show you mine." Jake knew he'd shocked her—it was what he'd intended doing—and it shocked him that she hadn't immediately jumped and ran. Wasn't she insulted by such a crude request? *Don't tell me she's actually considering doing it!*

Then his mouth dropped open, because she had started untying the sash. He was the one to jump up, and he bent over her and laid his hand on hers. "Carly, don't. I didn't mean it."

She tipped her head to look into his eyes. "But you'd like it, wouldn't you?"

He licked his dry lips. "That's not the point. Carly, try to understand. I can't do this. I will not jeopardize my relationship with your dad for a summer fling."

"A summer fling," she repeated quietly. "Yes, I suppose that's all it could ever be. But I'll tell you something, Jake. I've never really enjoyed sex before, but I enjoyed it with you. How do I forget what you made me feel? If I'm contented with a summer fling and Dad never finds out about it—although I'm positive he wouldn't care if he did learn of it—where's the harm? You and I sleep alone in this house. In fact, no one else ever comes into it, even during the day. Think of the kind of summer we could have.''

He stared into her eyes and felt his resolve slipping away. She was talking about uncountable joys, of making love anytime they felt like it. No one did come into the house, not at night, not during the day. He could open her robe this second, and caress her satiny skin, and kiss every inch of her body, and…and…

He pushed himself up and away from her chair. ''No,'' he said harshly. ''Now, go and put on some clothes or find some other damn fool to badger.''

Carly slowly stood up. ''You are a damn fool, Banyon,'' she said with a derisive twist of her lips. ''No wonder you're the most miserably unhappy person I've ever seen.'' She swept from the room.

Jake stared after her with a startled expression. He wasn't miserably unhappy. Why would she say something like that?

Carly stayed in the robe just to show Jake she'd do as she damn well pleased. She got out the vacuum cleaner and put a new bag into it, then set to work in the dingy, dusty living room. She only stopped cleaning for some lunch around one, and by four the living room was as clean as anyone could get it without a bucket of paint or some new wallpaper.

Actually, it looked great, and Carly sat on the fresh-smelling sofa and admired her handiwork. Her fancy robe was dirty, as she herself was, but the room fairly sparkled. Obviously Jake had left the house at some point, but she'd been trying very hard not to think about him.

Instead, she'd concentrated on the stallion and the mares, and where in this vast land the herd might now be grazing. Were they even on the ranch anymore?

She had to find them again, that's all there was to it. If Jake or his men did, that stallion would be dog food!

When Jake went into the house after supper that night he saw a piece of paper taped to the frame of the door between the kitchen and the hallway that led to the staircase to the second floor. Obviously Carly had written him a note and put it in a spot he couldn't possibly miss.

He took it down and read it.

Jake.

I'm going riding early again tomorrow morning. I prefer riding in the early hours and I also prefer riding alone. So do not set anyone on my trail. If I even catch a glimpse of anyone following me, I promise to raise more hell than you'd care to deal with.

Carly

Jake mumbled a curse and crumpled the note into a wad, which he then tossed into the trash can. Checking the time, he decided it wasn't too late to call Stuart. He went to the office, sat at the desk and dialed Stuart's number. He answered on the third ring.

"Stu, I hope I'm not disturbing you."

"Not at all. Jake, is Carly all right?"

"She's fine. But this call is about her. I'd like someone to go with her when she goes riding, but she insists on being alone. In fact, the other day I assigned the job of sticking close to her to Deke Johnson, and Carly raised holy hell over it. Told me she didn't need a baby-sitter. Stu, I'm concerned about her riding too far away from the compound one day and getting lost. How do you feel about it? Am I worrying for nothing?"

"I wouldn't say that," Stuart said slowly. "I wonder why she wants to ride alone. Deke or one of the other men didn't say something to her they shouldn't have, did they?"

Jake's heart skipped a beat. "No, they didn't. She eats with the men once in a while and she seems to get along with them just fine. From what I've seen, they're friendly but polite with her, just as they should be."

"I'm not sure how to look at this, Jake. She sounds just great when we talk on the phone…happier than she's been in a long time. Not so tense, if you know what I mean. Maybe she's finding the ranch tranquilizing. She could be doing a lot of thinking during her solitary rides. Or, Jake, is it possible that she's looking for that stallion and would prefer your not knowing about it? Carly's always been an animal lover. When she was a little girl she hauled home every stray cat and dog she could find."

A chill went up Jake's spine. He'd let Carly believe that he intended to shoot the stallion if and when the horse was ever captured, and he should have set her straight on that the first day she got to the ranch. He had to tell her the truth, and he had to do it tonight!

"That could be it. I'll have a talk with her before I go to bed."

"Good idea."

After goodbyes, Jake sat there stunned. He'd made too many mistakes with Carly. Now he had to undo them, he had to. Good Lord, if she was out looking for that stallion, anything could happen. What if she ran into a grizzly bear? The area wasn't overrun with grizzlies, but every so often someone spotted one.

Pushing his chair away from the desk, Jake got up and crossed the room to the door, where he switched off the lights and then headed for the stairs. On the second floor he hurried down the hall and stopped at the door to Carly's room. He knocked and called her name. "Carly?"

She was reading in bed and could hardly believe her ears. "What?" she shouted irritably. Did he dare to be in an on-again mood, the cad? She'd thrown herself at him that morning and been insultingly rebuffed. Did he think a woman ever forgot that sort of treatment from a man?

"I need to talk to you," Jake called through the door. "It's important."

"Well, I certainly doubt that," she yelled sarcastically.

"Carly, I have to talk to you!"

"Go away! I'm in bed."

"I'm not going away. I'm coming in."

"Don't you dare!" The door opened and Jake walked in. "You…you cretin!" she screeched, and she threw down her book to yank the covers up to her chin.

"Oh, for crying out loud," Jake said disgustedly. "Calm down. Today you tried every trick in the book to seduce me and now you're hollering because I'm in your bedroom. You're damned hard to understand, lady, damned hard."

"Well, don't tax your minuscule brain in trying. What do you want?"

"There's something I have to tell you." Jake picked up a chair and moved it closer to the bed. "I'm sure you don't mind if I sit down for this chat," he drawled.

"Cut to the chase, Banyon. What's so important it can't wait till tomorrow? And don't you dare tell me Deke or one of the other men is going with me in the morning, because they're not!" She shouted the last two words, then took a breath and spoke more normally. "I'm going riding alone tomorrow morning and any other day I decide to while I'm here, and you, especially, are not going to stop me!"

"What I have to tell you might stop you."

"What?" she said, suddenly terribly suspicious. And wary. What could he possibly have to tell her that would stop her from going riding alone? Then she knew. The stallion. They had found and killed the stallion. She began sobbing hysterically but she managed to choke out, "You…you bastard!"

Jake's jaw dropped. "Why am I a bastard? What brought that on? Carly, why are you crying?"

She couldn't lie still a second longer, and she threw back the covers. Jake gulped when he saw her short slip of a nightgown, and when she climbed out of bed he saw a lot more than that. No panties…again. His heart sank clear to his toes. How much of this could a man take before he broke down completely?

Carly brushed against Jake's knees as she pushed past him to pace the floor and bawl and berate him. "God's going to get you, don't you ever think he's not," she sobbed.

Jake got to his feet. "For what? Carly, I didn't do anything. I only came in here to talk. What in hell's going through your mind?"

"The stallion. You killed the stallion!"

"I did not!"

"Well, if you didn't do it, one of your…your henchmen did, you…you murderer! Deke told me he'd shoot the stallion if you asked him to, and you asked, didn't you? You had someone do it!"

"Good Lord," Jake said disgustedly. "Would you calm down enough to listen to me for three seconds? No one shot that stallion. No one's even seen him for days. The reason I came to your room was to apologize for letting you believe I ever intended killing that horse. It never was an option, but I…I let you think it was."

She stared at him for a long time, then yelled, "You're lying! You did plan to shoot him. You said so the day I got here."

"Only because you were so annoying," Jake said dryly.

"Because I was annoying? You self-centered jerk! What do you think you were? Still are, for that matter!"

"Probably annoying as hell. But answer me this, Carly, if you annoy me so much and I annoy you so much, how come we look at each other and think the word sex?"

"We don't! I don't, anyhow."

"Now who's lying? You're thinking it right now." Jake knew he should get out of her bedroom, but it was as if someone else had control of his body, and he moved toward her instead.

She watched him coming closer, and she quickly wiped the tears away from below her eyes. "You know I'm not going to say no, don't you?" she said huskily. "Even though I don't know that about you, you know it about me. That's not fair, Jake. It's so easy for you to resist me that I should be able to resist you the same way. Why can't I?"

"Don't ever think resisting you was easy for me." He pulled her into his arms, sighed in utter ecstasy and started kissing her. It felt so good to let go and do what had been driving him nuts since that day in the kitchen. And heaven knew he had her permission. She could not have made herself any clearer than she had today in the office. She wanted sex from him and she wanted it often.

Well, so did he, and it was time he faced his weakness for Carly Paxton and did what they both needed so badly.

"I'm going to love you senseless," he whispered. "Every morning, every night, during the day, in the middle of the night. You might as well move into my room."

Carly opened her mouth for his tongue and moaned. She wanted him so much that she hurt. His hands were under her short nightgown, caressing and stroking her buttocks, and it was pure magic...all of it.

Except for one thing. Gathering every ounce of strength she could find within the storm of longing battering her system, she pushed Jake away. He looked at her with dazed, questioning eyes.

"Not until I know for sure the stallion is still alive," she said breathlessly.

"How could you possibly know? Only God knows where he is. Carly, we're both on fire. You said today that we could have a fantastic summer, and we could, sweetheart, we could." He saw the determination and doubt in her eyes. "You still think I found the stallion and shot him, don't you?"

"If you didn't, where is he?" Carly walked over to the door and pulled it open. "I told you I couldn't say no, but I can. Please leave, Jake."

"Look, you're going to search for the stallion tomorrow, and so am I. Let's do it together."

She hesitated, then said, "No, I don't trust you."

"Dammit, I told you I never did plan to harm that thieving animal!"

"Well, forgive me if I can't quite overcome my doubt about that when you're so obviously furious about him stealing ranch mares."

"Hell, yes, I'm mad about it, but that doesn't make me an animal killer!"

"Doesn't it? I'm not so sure of that. Go to bed, Jake. You're getting nothing from me tonight."

"You're sentencing us both to getting nothing," he reminded her darkly.

"You think I don't know that? Produce the stallion, Jake, and we'll both be happy campers. In more ways than one. In a dozen ways. Go to bed and instead of counting sheep to fall asleep, count the various ways a man and a woman can make each other deliriously happy."

"You're a cruel woman, Carly."

"I learned how to be cruel from men, Jake. Good night."

Nine

Jake walked the floor of his bedroom, much too agitated to go to bed and count anything to fall asleep. There was more to the agony racking his body than simple lust, which gave him a whole slew of things to ponder. To Jake lust *was* simple. It was purely physical and it never involved the heart. But while what he was suffering over Carly was certainly physical—Lord, had he ever wanted a woman more?—his heart, soul and emotions seemed to be all tied up into one huge knot.

He tried desperately to find the key that would unlock that knot, because it seemed to be squeezing the breath out of him, and he kept pacing, frowning and stewing over it.

Nothing was right anymore. That damned stallion stealing mares had been bad enough, he sure hadn't had to heap stupidity onto adversity by falling for his boss's daughter!

Regardless, Carly should not be traipsing all over four-thousand acres, by herself, looking for that stallion. It wasn't safe, dammit, it wasn't! And she was so blasted stubborn about anyone going with her.

Jake narrowed his eyes as an idea began taking shape in his brain. Yes, that could be the answer, he thought as the idea expanded and took on clarity. The only way Carly would ever learn about it was if she ran into some kind of trouble out there by herself. Then she would discover that she hadn't been alone at all, but if she needed help and someone magically appeared, she wouldn't be angry, she'd be thankful.

Striding purposefully from his room, Jake stopped to knock on Carly's door again. "What time are you going riding in the morning?" he called.

Carly had been lying in bed, staring at the ceiling with the nightstand lamp on and her book next to her, totally forgotten. But how could she enjoy fiction when her own life had more twists and turns than the story she'd been reading? For one, who could ever have guessed that she would fall in love in Wyoming? Her father had sent her there to get over her miserable marriage and divorce. She had not been nearly as bad off as Stuart had worried about. She'd agreed to the trip to make him feel better.

Now she was up to her eyeballs involved with a man who kept worrying about his dumb job. Hell's bells, didn't Jake know her dad at all? If she was happy, her father was happy, and since he already liked Jake so much, where was the problem? Oh, sure, Jake would carry on an affair with her this summer, but she knew in her soul that he would swear her to secrecy. It was just plain silly, that's what it was.

Sighing, Carly reached out to turn off the lamp, and that was when she heard Jake's knock and question.

"Why do you want to know?" she asked, suspicious of what he might have thought up now to keep her under someone's watchful eye.

"Only because if I hear you at three in the morning again, I won't have to get up and make sure some sneak thief isn't hauling off everything that isn't nailed down."

"Oh. Well, I guess that makes sense. I won't be getting up until five, so I should be leaving around five-thirty."

"Okay, thanks. See you tomorrow when you get back."

Carly frowned and muttered, "Well, aren't you just one surprise after another?" Obviously Jake had accepted her determination to go riding alone, even though he knew now that she was not just ambling along on her horse but looking for the stallion. How irritating.

You could have spent the whole day with him tomorrow, you know. He suggested you join forces to search for the stallion, if you'd care to remember.

"Oh, shut up," she mumbled at her annoying inner voice, switching off the lamp.

Jake made one more stop before leaving the house. From a cupboard in the office, he lifted out a good-sized box. After checking its contents and making sure all batteries were fully charged, he took the box, left the house and headed for the men's quarters, the bunkhouse.

He walked in, set the box on a table and spoke to the curious faces of the men still up and those who were getting out of bed to see what their boss wanted. "We've got a special job tomorrow. All of us, except for Barney. Everyone is to take one of these two-way radios so we can stay in touch." Jake walked over to a map of the ranch on the wall. "Carly Paxton plans to leave the compound around five-thirty in the morning. We'll leave an hour earlier. Barney, we'll need an early breakfast and sandwiches to take with us. Each man is to see to his own water supply.

"Joe, I want you staked out at Logan's Creek. Conceal yourself and your horse in the trees. Pete, you go to this hill and use the heavy brush to keep out of sight." Jake pointed at a spot on the map, and one by one, he assigned every man a location with a view.

"I'll be trailing behind Carly, far enough behind that she doesn't catch on. Each of you will keep me informed, by radio, of her exact route."

It was Barney who asked the questions everyone was thinking. "What's going on, Jake? Are you afraid she'll get lost again?"

"She hasn't been out riding almost everyday for the love of the sport, Barney, she's been looking for that stallion. What if she catches sight of him and follows? There's some mighty treacherous ground out there, and she has no idea of what she could run into."

One of the men snickered. "If she runs into a grizzly she'll change her tune."

Jake shot him a dirty look. "If you ran into a grizzly, Hopper, you might be a little more considerate of a greenhorn's attitude toward this country." Jake looked each man in the eye. "Does everyone understand what we'll be doing tomorrow? And let me add that it might not be just tomorrow. I'm going to keep on trying to talk Carly out of worrying about that stallion, but as long as she does, we're going to protect her."

"Without her knowing about it," Deke Johnson murmured.

"That's right, Deke, without her knowing about it. I want her watched wherever she might go on this ranch, and I think there are enough of us to do that. If and when she passes your post, you are to quietly call me on the radio. I'll take it from there. Any questions?"

"Nope."

Jake left the bunkhouse satisfied that each man would do his job tomorrow. As for regular ranch chores, they would just have to be put on hold. Carly's life was far more important than anything else right now, and Jake honestly believed her life could be at stake. She really didn't have any idea of what she might run into if she got lost again and wandered too far from the compound.

He was not going to let that happen, and he wasn't doing this for Stu and maybe not even for Carly. It was for himself.

He would hate himself forever if he did nothing and Carly got hurt—or worse.

When the alarm went off at five the next morning, Carly sat up and turned off the buzzer. Yawning, she put her feet on the floor and asked herself if this was really necessary. Wouldn't it be easier to believe that Jake didn't intend to harm the stallion and let it go at that? She could sleep a few more hours, then get up at a reasonable time and do some more housecleaning.

But what if she *shouldn't* believe him? Frowning, Carly wondered why the stallion had moved the mares. Was it possible he had moved them back to the clearing since yesterday morning?

She at least had to check the clearing again. With that decision made and final, she got up from the bed, took her cosmetics case and headed for the bathroom and a shower.

Forty minutes later Carly was on horseback and riding west, toward the foothills. She turned in the saddle and looked behind her, because although she'd seen no one while saddling her horse, she felt now as though someone was nearby.

"Strange," she murmured, facing front again. Normally she was not unreasonably spooky, but she felt sort of eerie today, as though dozens of eyes were watching her every move. It was a ridiculous idea, of course, a feeling reminiscent of girlhood sleep-outs where everyone told ghostly, frightening stories and scared the living daylights out of themselves. Telling herself not to be so silly, she kept going.

Jake had the volume of his handheld radio turned down so he just barely heard his men's voices. "She's heading for the foothills, Jake." "She's riding up Baker Hill, Jake, just about to enter the pines." "Jake, she's in the trees. Can't see her anymore. What d'ya want me to do now?"

"Stay where you are, Joe. She might double back. I'll stay on her trail. I have an idea where she's going. Over and out."

Jake wondered why in hell she would keep going back to the place where the stallion had stolen Goldie right from under her butt, but that question only made him realize that Carly hadn't told him everything. He muttered under his breath, "And she probably never will, no matter how friendly the two of you might get." Women were such strange creatures, so difficult for a man to understand. Men and women didn't see things in the same way, and most of the time they might as well be talking two different languages for all the good a conversation between them did.

"Why'd the good Lord make us so different?" Jake mumbled. And then, for the first time in years, he thought of his mother. She had been a sweet, smiling woman with an iron will, and his father had been a man of steel with an underlying gentleness that few people got to see. And they had been happy with each other. In love with each other. So people didn't have to be alike to find that special magic that bonded them for life.

Jake felt a tear in his eye. How tragic that his mother had died so young and that his father had had to live without her for years and years.

"But who ever said life was fair?" Jake muttered emotionally.

Carly rode past the area where Goldie had thrown her, then on to the dry, rocky riverbed. There was probably a shorter route to get to the clearing, but that was the one Carly knew, which, she felt, was probably the quickest way for her in the long run because she wouldn't be wasting time by taking a wrong turn and having to do any backtracking. Actually, she felt quite confident with her sense of direction now, and perhaps one of these days she would find that shorter route to the clearing.

Like yesterday, however, there were no horses when Carly

got there—the stallion must have sensed danger here and
moved his ladies to a safer location. Disappointed enough to
cry, Carly rode her horse in a circular pattern and wondered
what might have alarmed the stallion. Had the men Jake sent
out everyday to look for the stallion gotten too close to this
pretty meadow among the pines? What else would frighten
a stallion—a bear? A grizzly?

Carly looked around with sudden wariness and pulled her
horse to a stop. It was so quiet. Had it been this quiet out
here yesterday? Why was she feeling goose bumps on her
arms?

With her eyes darting this way and that, she took a drink
of water from her canteen. Something or someone was
watching her, dammit, this eerie feeling was not just her
imagination! What if it was a grizzly?

"Oh, Lord," she whispered, and quickly hooked the
leather loop of the canteen around the saddle's pommel again
and got her horse moving. But reason cut her frantic, fearful
flight short. She'd had the same "watched" feeling near the
compound, and there certainly had not been a grizzly bear
there! Goodness, she was behaving like a child in the dark.

Jake wondered what in heck was going on with Carly. The
clearing she was in—she was riding in stops and starts, as
though she was really jumpy about something—looked interesting. Large animals had recently grazed the grass, of that
he had no doubt. But until Carly moved out, he couldn't
move in to get a better look. Then and only then would he
know *which* large animals were using this place for food and
asylum.

Carly was debating. It looked to her as though there was
a crude trail on the far side of the meadow, possibly one that
the stallion might have taken to move the mares. Why, the
herd could be in the very next clearing, assuming there was
a "next clearing," of course. But could she follow a strange
trail with only the sun as a positional gauge?

Was there any reason she couldn't follow a strange trail?

After all, she was hardly the totally ignorant little greenhorn she'd been when she'd gotten here! Yes, the thought of running into a grizzly was scary, but it would be scary to anyone with a lick of good sense. All she had to do was keep her head and stay alert to possible pitfalls and danger.

She could do it, she knew she could! Turning her horse's head, she headed for the obscure trail in the trees.

"Carly, Carly, where are you going now?" Jake mumbled from the opposite side of the clearing. The pine forest just got thicker and more dense in the direction Carly was riding. But maybe she had picked up a clue in this clearing that led her to believe that she was getting close to the stallion and mares.

When she was out of sight, Jake rode his horse into the clearing and was almost immediately amazed by what he was seeing. *This* was where the stallion had been keeping his harem! And Carly had somehow stumbled onto this place, actually seen the herd with her own eyes, then kept it from everyone to protect the stallion.

"Damn!" Jake exclaimed angrily, recalling the night she'd eaten supper with the men and the way he'd wondered why she had looked so smug. That was probably the day she'd found this spot, and if he hadn't been such a horse's patoot and let her believe that he just might shoot the stallion when he captured him, she probably would have come to him and told him of her discovery. They'd already have the mares back, and today he wouldn't have every man on the place tracking Carly to make sure she didn't break her fool neck.

But she wasn't the fool, he was! He pushed the talk button on his radio. "Deke, can you hear me?"

"Just barely, Jake."

"That's 'cause I'm in the woods. Carly's heading south. If she stays on course, she will end up on federal land and possibly come out of the trees near that big hot spring. I'm going to stay on her trail. I want you to radio each of the other men and position them so they've all got a good view of the foothills. If she comes out of the pines at any point, I want to know about it at once. Over and out.''

''Okay, Jake. Over and out.''

Nudging his horse with his knees, Jake headed him toward that little gap in the trees that Carly had vanished through.

The sun had disappeared. All Carly could see of the sky were some thin, high clouds, just enough of them to conceal the sun. Carly told herself not to panic, but it was evident that she was now without any sort of directional guide at all.

Except for one thing. She was positive that she was tracking the stallion and mares! There were signs—horse droppings, hoof marks, places where the grass had been cropped off or stomped down—and she couldn't give up and retrace or 'attempt to retrace' her own trail. It would be nothing short of a miracle if she found that glorious horse and his harem for a second time. But it could happen, and Carly felt as though it was going to happen.

But it certainly wouldn't happen if she panicked and gave up at this crucial point. So what if the day was passing? Surely this would all be over before dark.

Carly's legs and back ached from being in the saddle for so many hours. Her watch indicated 4:10 p.m.; it was nearing the dinner hour. In her mind's eye she saw the ranch. Jake would be going into the house for his shower, and the men would be cleaning up and gathering at the cookhouse for one of Barney's good meals. Would any of them notice that she hadn't gotten back from her ride?

''Probably not,'' Carly said with a sigh. Since she rarely showed herself in the men's dining room, why would anyone miss her? ''But you'll be back before dark,'' she bravely told herself out loud. It was something she had to keep telling herself, because in the back of her mind she knew that she had ridden quite a distance from the ranch's buildings.

All of a sudden, without a dram of warning, Carly was in the open. She had ridden right out of the trees, and before

her were all sorts of strange-looking machinery and structures. "It's a mining operation," she said under her breath.
"Or, rather, it was a mining operation." Now, everything
was rusty and ramshackle, obviously long-deserted.

But whoever owned this property still didn't want anyone
on it because there were several large No Trespassing signs
in plain sight.

Carly peered at the gray sky and tried to get her bearings.
She had to be somewhere south of the ranch, but she could
be southwest or southeast. And which way was directly
north?

She was still pondering that serious question—and worrying a little—when she saw a stirring sight, the stallion and
mares, grazing peacefully on the other side of the old mine.

She'd found them. How incredible. Feeling as though she
had discovered the pot of gold at the end of the rainbow,
Carly dismounted and led her horse over to one of the ancient
buildings that was part of the old mining operation. Maybe
there would be some kind of clue as to her exact location in
one of these structures, she reasoned as she tethered her
horse, then tried the door. It was locked, and so was every
other building.

"Okay, so much for that idea. Let's see now. It's starting
to get dark, and I'm about a thousand miles from the ranch
and I have only a little water in my canteen and no food left,
so I guess everything's just peachy," she drawled sardoni-
cally, refusing to let herself get all crazed and scared yet.
Maybe later, but not yet.

Spotting one more very tiny building across some rubble,
Carly left her horse behind and strode toward it. She was
walking on some old boards, thinking no more of them than
she had of the rocks she'd just been on, when they crumbled
and she felt herself falling. Landing hard at the bottom of a
deep hole, with her left ankle twisted beneath her, she felt
true fear.

"Oh, no," she moaned. No one would ever find her here.

There wasn't even any point to yelling for help because there was no one to hear her.

Jake had seen the whole thing, and when Carly disappeared he thought his own heart might stop. But he couldn't worry about himself. Carly could be seriously injured.

Jake knew exactly where they were, and at least three of his crew members were within a quarter mile of this spot, because he'd kept in radio contact and made sure they knew where he was. Actually, they weren't that far from the ranch, not in miles. Carly's circuitous route through the foothills had taken up the day, but a direct ride back to the ranch shouldn't take more than an hour.

Kicking his horse in the ribs, he ran the animal as near to the spot where Carly had vanished as was possible. Then he leaped to the ground and ran over to the hole.

Kneeling, he peered over the edge. "Carly? Are you all right? Can you hear me? Can you talk to me?"

She opened her eyes and looked up. "Jake? What are you doing here?"

"I'll tell you later. Are you hurt?"

"Just my ankle. I think it might be sprained."

"And that's all? Nothing's broken?"

"No, I'm fine, except for my left ankle."

"Carly, are you absolutely positive? I don't want to move you if there's a chance…"

"Good grief, I'm fine!" To prove it, she hung onto a protruding board and pulled herself up to stand on her right foot. "Do you believe me now?"

"Yes. Okay, I'm going to go get a rope and then get you out of there. I'll only be gone a few minutes, so don't be scared, all right?"

"I'm not scared," she said a bit impatiently. "I'm more interested in what you're doing here than I am in a barely sprained ankle, for heaven's sake. Jake, why are you here?"

"To save your life, why else?" Jake got up and ran back to his horse. Instead of immediately taking the rope that was tied behind the saddle, he talked into his radio. "Deke, are you there?"

"Sure am, Jake. What's happening?"

"I'm at the old Haywood mine. So is Carly. Incidentally, the stallion and mares are grazing on the other side of the mine, paying me no mind at all."

"You're kidding. You found the stallion?"

"Carly did. I'm just an onlooker," Jake said a bit cynically, then altered his tone of voice. "He really is a fine-looking animal, Deke. And the mares don't look any worse for wear. Listen, Carly and I will be heading back in about fifteen minutes. She has a slight injury, so I want her back at the ranch as soon as possible. In the meantime, I'd like you to round up two or three of the other men and bring our mares home. You're going to have to play it by ear with the stallion. At first sight of men on horseback, he'll probably bolt and run, so catch him if you can, but don't worry about it if you can't. It's the mares that are important."

"I understand. Anything else?"

"I think that about covers it. Just play it safe, Deke, and we'll have those mares back where they belong tonight. Over and out."

Tucking the radio into a saddlebag, Jake untied the rope from behind the saddle and hurried back to the hole in the moldy old boards. "Carly, I'm going to toss down a rope. Tie it around your waist and I'll bring you up."

"You're going to lift me all that way? I don't think so, Jake. I am not a lightweight."

"Just try it without arguing, okay? If that doesn't work, I'll come down there and get you. One way or another, you're going to be out of that hole in short order."

"Before you do one thing," she shouted up at him, "I want to know how you so conveniently happened to be here."

"Carly, just shut your sexy mouth for once in your life, and tie the end of this rope around your waist!"

"My *sexy* mouth? Jake, have you been following me all day?"

"Good Lord, the woman never knows when to shut up. Carly, tie the damn rope!"

It took a few minutes, but finally Carly was out of the hole. Teetering on her good foot, she willingly put her hands on Jake's shoulders while he untied the rope around her waist.

"Thank you," she said quietly. "If you hadn't followed me, Lord only knows how long I would have been down there. But I'd still like to know—have to know—the reason you gave up your entire day just to see where I was going. Did you think I knew something that you didn't?"

He looked directly into her eyes. "You did, didn't you? You knew exactly where the stallion and mares had been hiding out." Carly looked back at him, but said nothing, then they both looked across the old mining machinery at the stallion and mares.

"They're so beautiful," she said emotionally.

"Yes," Jake agreed, "they are." He brought his gaze back to her and spoke huskily. "You're what's beautiful, Carly."

She saw the smoky, simmering light in his eyes and knew precisely what he was thinking about. Her pulse began beating faster. "You're kind of beautiful yourself," she whispered. She was suddenly so full of sexual tension that she would have lain down in the dirt for him, if he so much as hinted she should.

Instead he got himself together and said, almost gruffly, "Come on, let's hop you over to that old bench so you can sit down. I want to examine your ankle and see how badly it's sprained."

"It's really not that bad," Carly murmured. But she gladly leaned on his strength to reach the bench, and she smiled adoringly at him when he knelt before her.

"I would repeat what I said before, that big brave statement of not needing a baby-sitter, if you hadn't just proved that maybe I do need a keeper in this country," she said softly.

Jake gently probed her foot and ankle through her boot, and she winced only a little. "Everyone does out here, Carly, and it's nothing to be ashamed of, either. It's the isolation. Incidents that wouldn't mean beans in a populated area can be disastrous out here."

"The fall I took down that hole, for instance."

"Exactly. I'm going to leave your boot on, because once it's off, your ankle is likely to swell. Let's get you on your horse so we can head for home. You need some ice for that sprain, and I think you should try to stay off of that foot for at least a day."

"Yes, doctor," Carly said with a teasing light in her eyes. "Jake, you can be so nice. How come you walk around with a scowl on that handsome face most of the time?"

He took her hands and gently pulled her up from the bench. She anticipated immediately being led to her horse, but instead he wrapped his arms around her and looked into her eyes. "One kiss, then we'll go," he murmured in a way that set her heart to racing.

She offered her lips, parted, moist and sensual, and felt the approach of his clear to the tips of her toes.

In that very instant a sharp cracking noise punctured the quiet, intruding on the peace and tranquillity of this old deserted mining area. It startled Carly so much that she broke away from Jake as though their nearness to each other was the obscenity that someone was shooting at!

But she knew at once that she wasn't the target, nor was Jake—the stallion was!

Her eyes filled with tears, but she still saw the stallion go down, catch himself and then get up and start running. The mares followed, and the little herd raced away, out of sight in seconds.

Teetering on her right foot, she turned her teary eyes on Jake and whispered hoarsely, "You bastard! You had him shot!"

Ten

Carly was furious and inconsolable. She wouldn't let Jake help her walk to her horse, nor get on it. She managed it all in stiff-lipped, teary-eyed fury, and whenever Jake tried to talk to her during the ride back to the ranch, she cut him off with some unforgiving rebuff.

"Carly, I swear to you that…"

"Don't worsen your sinful behavior by lying, too," she snapped.

"But you can't condemn me without…"

"Like hell I can't! I saw the evidence of your treachery with my own eyes, you cold-hearted jerk! How was that stallion hurting you? You don't own the mares he's taken, my dad does! I want that stallion found and I want him treated by a vet. I swear to God if he dies from that bullet wound, I will badger Dad until he fires every man on the place, including you!"

That did it for Jake. He would beg no more. He prayed that the stallion wasn't fatally wounded, not because of

Carly's fury but because he himself was sick at heart over the incident. One of his men had fired that shot, but which man? And why, for God's sake?

Carly noticed that Jake was no longer pleading with her, and she wondered which of her gems of outrage had shut him up. Not that it mattered. How could she possibly have thought she was in love with him? Any man who could do what he had today didn't deserve the love of a good woman.

"May he rot in hell," she muttered, then feeling fresh tears sting her eyes. *Damn him! I do still love him!* "God help me," she whispered, disappointed in herself.

Halfway to the ranch they met up with Deke and two other men. "Who fired that shot?" Jake demanded brusquely.

"Don't know, Jake. We heard it, but we didn't see who did it. Did it do any damage?"

"It sent the stallion and mares flying," Jake said disgustedly. "They're probably in the next county by now. I'm going to find out who did it, Deke, and when I do…" He let that idea dangle and said instead, "Come on, we might as well all go home. For now."

Barney delivered an ice pack and a plate of food to Carly's room. She had changed into a nightgown and was in bed, so when she heard Barney call, "Ms. Paxton? Is it all right if I come in?" she hurriedly made sure the blankets were up past her bosom because her nightgown was rather revealing and called back, "Yes, Barney, please do."

He walked in juggling the plate—covered by a napkin—and the ice pack. "I'll bet you're hungry," he said, setting the plate on the dresser. "But before you eat, let's take a look at that ankle."

Carly pulled back the blankets over her feet and watched Barney's face as he examined her sore ankle. "It's not too bad," he told her. "Should be fine in a day or two. Better to elevate it, though. Hand me that extra pillow." He placed her foot on the pillow, then the ice pack so that it was up against the swelled area of her ankle.

"It should be iced about fifteen minutes of every hour," Barney told her, then grinned. "We don't want to freeze your ankle, just to get rid of some of that swelling."

"This is awfully nice of you, Barney," she said. "Thank you. I really hate being a bother."

"Stuff and nonsense," Barney exclaimed. "You ain't no bother at all. Now, I brought you a nice plate of supper, and I'll run down to the kitchen and get you anything you'd like to drink. How about a nice glass of milk?" Barney snapped his fingers. "Almost forgot. Hold on a second, and I'll be right back."

He hurried out and was back in no time with a bed tray. "Jake used this when he hurt his back two summers ago. It should work just fine for your meals." Barney set the tray up across Carly's hips. "How's that?" he asked. "Does it fit okay? Should I put the plate on it? Are you comfortable?"

Carly smiled. "I'm very comfortable, Barney, thank you. Yes, put the plate on the tray and then, if you really don't mind, I would love a glass of milk."

Nodding, Barney hurried out again. Carly lifted the napkin on the huge plate—it was closer to the size of a platter than an ordinary dinner plate—and saw slices of roast beef, a mouthwatering array of vegetables and a mound of fresh fruit salad. There was also a knife and fork.

"Barney, you're a sweetheart," she said softly. Then she sighed, heavily. She had gotten off her horse by herself, simply dropped the reins because she really hadn't cared who might tend the animal, and then limped to the house under her own steam. She hadn't worried about food or an ice pack or just how she would get along all on her own, so Barney was really a lifesaver.

He returned with a tall glass of milk and a handful of napkins. "Forgot those," he said with a little grin. "Okay, now here's something else." From his back pocket he pulled out a little black gadget that looked to Carly like a cellular telephone. "This here is a two-way radio," he told her. "Leave it on channel fourteen. That's the one we use on the ranch. You and me can stay in touch this way, so if you need something and can't get it yourself, just let me know."

Carly accepted the radio and looked it over. "And how do I use it? Oh, I see. This is the talk button. Do I release it when you're talking?"

"Yeah, that's it exactly. You're a smart lady. The radio is on now, and I'd like you to leave it on in case I want to check on you and hear how you're doing. Okay? Are you all set now?"

"How can I ever thank you for all this, Barney? I didn't expect it, that's for sure."

"Well, Jake asked me to keep an eye on you, and you know, ma'am, he really feels bad about what happened."

Carly's smile faded. "Only because he got caught in a very despicable act, Barney. I'll say good-night now, because after I eat I'm going to go right to sleep."

"Uh, good night."

After Barney had gone, Carly hoped that she hadn't hurt his feelings, but it was obvious that Jake had poor Barney completely snowed.

To think that he had been right behind her all day! Small wonder she'd gotten the heebie-jeebies and felt as though she was being watched. She *was* being watched, by Jake Banyon! He must have figured out that she'd known where the stallion was, and then he'd set up the whole awful scenario so one of his men could get a rifle bead on that beautiful horse. What a disappointment it must have been for Jake that it hadn't been an instant kill.

"Oh, stop dwelling on it," she told herself irately. It had been an awful day, but there was nothing she could do about it tonight. She couldn't even go back downstairs and call her father, as Jake had been right. Once she'd taken off her boot, her ankle had ballooned, and while the ice was helping, it

hurt a lot more without the support of the boot than it had
with it.

*Why in hell don't these bedrooms have telephones? This
house is hopelessly outdated. Why didn't Dad ever have it
modernized?*

*Probably because Jake is so outdated himself he doesn't
even notice the inconveniences all around him. He's probably so behind the times that if Dad did suggest any improve-
ments, Jake would stumble over his own tongue and stammer,
"Gosh... shucks...heck no, Stu. Everything's just fine as it
is."*

"He's not a hayseed, so don't kid yourself about that,"
Carly mumbled at herself, finally picking up her fork and
starting to eat. What, exactly, was Jake's history? she mused
during the delicious meal. Had he ever been married? In
love? Engaged? Did he have children? Parents? Brothers or
sisters? Where was he from? Where had he grown up? If he
had family, where did they live now?

In all honesty, she saw Banyon as an orphan, someone
with no family at all, and no friends, either. But why did he
live that way? No one could help not having family, but that
wasn't true of friends.

Well, she wasn't that great in the friends department herself, she thought with a sigh. She used to have a lot of
friends, but that was before her ex had all but isolated them
from the rest of the world so no one would catch on to what
a louse he really was. But why think of that now? she asked
herself. *Every chapter of a person's life seems to have its
own brand of problems. You've got enough to worry about
in the present without rehashing the past.*

Darn it, she really wanted a telephone. Her dad should
know what was going on here, and she sincerely doubted that
Jake would tell his boss about the incident from anyone's
point of view but his own. Which, she was positive, would
make him look like a hero and her like a hysterical female.

Carly knew she was getting herself into a lather again, but

keeping a lid on her anger just wasn't possible. If she only knew how badly the stallion had been wounded. Dammit, if she only knew something! For instance, what were Jake and his crew of thugs doing tonight, celebrating?

Frustration over being immobile made Carly clench her teeth. Throwing caution to the wind, she reasoned that she had made it up the stairs by herself, so she should be able to go back down the stairs. To test her theory Carly maneuvered the food tray from the bed to the floor. Her ankle protested the movement with a sharp jab of pain, fueling her anger because it was pretty darned obvious that she was stuck right where she was.

Giving up for the time being, but not without resentment, she lay back on her pillow. Staying in bed for a day or two, as Barney had indicated, was a horrible prospect. She would go mad without the mobility to come and go as she pleased.

And then, from the two-way radio came Barney's voice. "Are you all right, Miss Paxton?"

She pushed the talk button. "Barney, *please* call me Carly. And no, I'm not all right, but until this ankle heals the only thing I can do about it is complain. Barney, are you alone?"

"Alone in the kitchen, ma'am. What would you like, some dessert?"

"No! I mean, no, thanks. I just feel so out of the loop up here alone. I think I'd even talk civilly to Jake if he came along right now, and that's saying a lot because I will never get over him ordering someone to shoot that stallion. Barney, did all the men come in for dinner? Did anyone know how badly the stallion was injured?"

"No one was here for supper, Carly. Jake's got the whole crew out tracking the stallion. I wouldn't doubt that they'll be out all night."

"Oh, no," Carly moaned. "They're going to make darn sure he's dead, aren't they? Barney, doesn't anyone have a cellular phone on this place?"

"There's no cellular service way out here, Carly. Do you need a phone for something?"

"Yes, I do."

"Well, there's one in Jake's room. Would ya like me to come to the house and help you hop from your bedroom to his?"

A phone in Jake's room? Hell's bells, I can hop that far on my own! "Thanks, Barney, but I'm sure I can get that far by myself. I really am fine so please don't worry. I'll see you tomorrow."

"Good night and sleep well. Oh, I'll take the radio to bed with me and leave it on, so if you need anything in the night, just give me a call. Over and out."

"Over and out," Carly said, repeating Barney's sign-off. Laying down the radio, she carefully sat up and slid back the blankets. Very slowly she inched her sore ankle from the pillow to the edge of the bed. It hurt, it hurt like hell, but she was going to get to that telephone if she had to crawl.

Gingerly, moving at a snail's pace, she got turned on the bed so that her feet were on the floor. The blood rushing to her sprained ankle made her cry out. "Oh, damn, that hurts!"

But she was determined to get to that phone, and she gritted her teeth and forced herself up to her right foot. Hopping, however, proved to be most ineffective. Every bounce to her bad ankle made her want to scream, and, all in all, hopping was a lot harder work than she'd supposed.

Okay, fine, I'll crawl! She got down on her hands and knees. Her first discovery in that position was that the skirt of long nightgown was an awful hindrance. *Darn it, even a short gown would be in the way. Or a nightshirt. Anything that hangs down.*

To hell with it. There's no one to see you naked, so get on with it! Plopping her behind on the carpet, she pulled the nightgown over her head, then started crawling again. *Ah, much better.*

In no time she was down the hall and reaching up to turn

the knob on Jake's bedroom door. She pushed the door open and peered into the dark room. Obviously she was going to have to locate a light switch, and she used the door frame to pull herself up to her good foot again. And there, right next to the frame was a switch. She pushed it and the bedside lamp came on.

To her surprise, Jake's bed was neatly made. But much more interesting than that tidbit of information was the telephone next to the lamp on the bed stand.

Carly hopped her way over to the bed, yanked back the top blanket to use as a cover-up and dropped onto the bed like a sack of potatoes, totally exhausted. Tucking the blanket around herself, she picked up the phone and dialed her father's New York number. She got his voice mail.

Daddy, I fell in a hole and sprained my ankle. I'm probably going to have to stay in bed for days and days. Jake had the stallion shot, and you're not home, and I don't have anyone to talk to, and...and...why aren't you home when I need you?

"Hi, Dad. It's just me, checking in. I keep forgetting the three-hour time differential between Wyoming and New York. No need to hurry to call me back. I really only wanted to say hello. Obviously you're out somewhere, and I hope it's not all business. Good night. I love you."

Carly put down the phone, then laid her head on Jake's pillow. She would shut her eyes for just a minute, then crawl back to her own room. She could not...remember...of ever...being so...worn out...so...completely done...in...

The second Jake reached the top of the stairs he saw the lights coming from Carly's room and his room. The doors to both rooms had to be open, but why would they be?

He became wary and sidled noiselessly along the wall until he came to Carly's bedroom, then he quickly peeked into the room around the door frame. The lamp was on, and the bed was empty. Frowning, he pondered the situation. She should not only be in her room, she should be in bed. Off her bad ankle. So…where was she? And why were the lights on in *his* room?

No, she would never go to his room, he told himself when that possibility arose in his mind. Or would she? Had she thought things over, realized that he was not the villain she'd accused him of being and gotten over her anger? It seemed to be a perfectly logical explanation of why she would be in his room, and it cheered Jake. In fact it did a little more than cheer him, it started his blood racing and his heart pounding, because if Carly was waiting for him in his bedroom, she must have loving on her mind.

Jake had walked into the house tired out from the long day. It was after midnight, and the only thing on *his* mind had been a good night's sleep—or at least five hours' sleep.

But now—just because Carly was apparently waiting for him in his room—he suddenly wasn't tired at all. A man's recuperative powers because of a woman were downright amazing.

But there was another power at work between him and Carly, and it was even more amazing—the power of a physical attraction neither of them could really overcome, though each of them had tried at various times.

Jake tiptoed down the hall, positive that Carly had some sort of surprise in store for him—difficult with a sprained ankle but not impossible—and with each step he took his excitement grew.

"Carly, sweetheart," he said as he rounded the door frame with a beaming smile and enough eager anticipation to fill a boxcar. He stopped just inside the room and felt his smile fading away. Other than one delectable bare leg and the top of her head, she was completely hidden under a blanket— the blanket he used as a spread on his bed!

He didn't know what to think…or do…but then he slowly walked to the edge of the bed and lifted a corner of the blanket to see her face. "Sweetheart, are you really sleeping?"

She never budged, and he could tell by her shallow breathing that she was indeed sleeping. She was in a very deep sleep, in fact. He sighed rather sadly, because here she was—obviously having come to his room to wait for him to get back so they could kiss and make up. Oh, what an incredible image that idea provoked! And she hadn't been able to stay awake.

"It's all right, sweetheart," he whispered, and quickly began undressing. "You're here…signifying forgiveness…and that's enough." *I'll hold you in my arms and let you sleep, and maybe in the morning, when we're both refreshed…?*

He actually believed that was all that would happen if he crawled under that blanket with her. And he didn't stop believing it until he was down to his briefs and trying to adjust the blanket so there would be room for him next to her and he saw that she was stark naked.

His whole system went wild—she really had waited for him with loving on her mind! He pushed down his briefs, lay next to her, turned off the lamp and wound his arms around her.

His first feeling was profound tenderness. This beautiful, passionate woman had brought him back to life. He'd breathed in and out for four years, and had even judged himself contented, but he hadn't been. Not in ways that mattered. Carly had turned his perspective of life, liberty and the pursuit of happiness completely upside down.

Okay, so she was also sassy, obstinate and defiant of any authority. Possibly, she listened to her dad, but Jake would bet that Stuart was the only person with opinions that might impress or influence Carly.

And yet she had feelings for him, for Jake Banyon. They were on-again, off-again feelings, granted, but when she was in "on" mood, things sizzled between them.

Refusing to ruin this rare and precious moment with guilty

thoughts of Stuart, Jake began moving his hands up and down the smooth, silky skin of Carly's back, hips and thighs. Pressing his lips to her forehead, he whispered, "I might never be able to say it in the light of day and when you're wide awake and looking at me, so I'll say it now. I love you. I love you more than life itself, and it's a miracle."

Carly was having the most incredible dream. It was very close to the dream she'd had her first night on the ranch, right after she'd met Jake for the first time, only this one was in more detail and much more erotic. She could actually feel his hands on her, and his naked body against hers. His manhood was hot and hard and pressed into her lower tummy, and he was whispering lovely words about his miraculous love for her.

Sighing sensually, she nestled closer and concentrated very hard on the dream so it wouldn't slip away from her consciousness and end up in that never-never land of forgotten dreams.

"Do it. Make love to me. Do it now. I need you so."

In her foggy, sleep-drugged brain Carly didn't know if she'd actually spoken or merely thought those things. It didn't seem to matter, because her dream lover was doing everything exactly right. His mouth adored hers with kisses so soft and gentle that she sank deeper into the dream, clung determinedly to its sweetness and symbolically hugged it around herself. She didn't dare lose it, she would die if she lost it.

On her back she felt him enter her, and for a fraction of a moment she almost came awake. In all of her life she had never dreamed of this, and in talking to girlfriends in the past, neither had they. Erotic dreams, yes, everyone had had them, but no one Carly knew had ever really experienced what she was experiencing now.

How incredible. How fantastic. It seemed so real. She could feel him inside her without feeling his weight on top of her! How could that be? Well, it was just a dream, for heaven's sake. Anything was possible.

And it was possible, she found out, to experience a climax so strong and overwhelmingly pleasurable that she lost the dream completely and everything went black.

· Jake reached his own pleasure peak and couldn't help crying out. "Carly! Baby!" Then, because she was so obviously sleeping again, and he was exhausted again, he simply put his arms around her, his head next to hers on the same pillow and fell asleep in two seconds.

Eleven

Jake woke at ten to five, and after lying there and remembering the glory of last night for a few minutes, he very gently—so he wouldn't disturb Carly—kissed her warm cheek and then slipped out of bed.

There was enough gray, predawn light coming through the windows to let him find clean clothes. Carrying everything, he tiptoed from the room, silently shut the door and went down the hall to use the other bathroom for a shower so Carly could sleep as long as she wanted.

Around seven Carly began stirring. With her eyes still closed, she stretched out her legs and felt a twinge in her left ankle. *It hardly hurts at all! Oh, thank goodness. I would have lost my mind staying in bed all day.*

What time is it? Opening her eyes, Carly's whole system went stiff. "My God," she moaned. "I slept in Jake's bed. But…but…"

She was suddenly warm all over. That hadn't been a dream

at all, it had been the real thing. Jake had come in late, found her in his bed and assumed she was there for...for sex! Waiting for him to come to bed to make love!

And he sure hadn't hesitated, had he? she thought angrily. But her anger dissipated a great deal when she realized that she didn't know if he'd hesitated or not. To be honest, she knew nothing of what had taken place last night except for some very torrid memories of a dream that hadn't been a dream at all, but instead had been the most exquisitely sensual experience of her life. "But he said that he loved me," she whispered, then frowned severely because she wasn't really positive that he'd said anything.

Had part of it been a dream and the other part real? Groaning, Carly buried her face in Jake's pillow. His scent filled her nostrils, and she bit down hard on her bottom lip. How in heaven's name could a woman sleep through the most thrilling sexual event of her life? Obviously she hadn't been a hundred percent asleep, but last night she'd thought she was.

And what had Jake thought? Recalling his hands on her, she became flushed and edgy, and not out of embarrassment, either. She wished Jake were still in bed with her and that he would do everything he'd done to her last night all over again. She would gladly stay in bed for a day or two if Jake would share it with her.

You dolt! All he did last night was take advantage of a situation you caused. Did he even try to wake you? Did he shake your arm and say, "Carly, wake up!" Did he do that and then ask what you were doing in his bed? No, he did not. He got into bed with you and touched you all over, and...and he had no right!

Turning over to her back, Carly stared at the ceiling and thought almost sadly. *He has the right. Anytime, anyplace, he has the right. No other man does, but Jake does. If I'd been wide awake last night, I would not have said no. He makes me feel things I never knew existed, and he makes me feel love when I sincerely believed I would never love again.*

"So," she murmured. "Where are you this morning, Mr. Banyon, and what are you and your band of horse murderers up to this fine day?" Had they found the stallion last night? Was that beautiful animal dead?

The luster of the sunshiny morning was suddenly gone for Carly. She had to find out what was going on, and no matter how deeply her feelings went for Jake, if the stallion was dead she would probably never be able to forgive and forget. In fact, her disappointment in Jake would be so profound, she might not even try.

While Carly hobbled around, took a shower and got dressed, the weather changed. The bright sunshine she had noticed coming through the windows of Jake's bedroom was being overcome by a fast-moving storm front. The wind was picking up velocity, and the gathering clouds indicated a typical Wyoming summer storm to Jake.

On horseback he talked into his radio. "This is Jake. Is anyone close enough to hear me?" The radios had a range of about a half mile.

"Joe here, Jake. I hear you loud and clear."

"This storm is moving in pretty fast, Joe. I'm going on but I want the rest of you to head back."

"Well, hell, Jake, we ain't made of sugar, either."

"Believe me, I know that," Jake said wryly. "But here's the deal. I'm coming up on Shell Canyon and I'm pretty sure that's where I'll find the stallion and mares."

"You've seen clear signs?"

"Lots of clear signs. Anyhow, there's only one way in and out of Shell Canyon, which means if those horses are there, they'll be easily caught. Not during a storm, though. I don't want the stallion to panic and hurt himself worse than he already is. All I plan to do today is take a look. And I don't need any help from you guys to do that. The thing is, I don't want anyone going off half-cocked if I don't get back by dark. I have a sleeping bag and some food and water with me. And there are a lot of caves in Shell Canyon, so if the storm turns into a gully-washer, I'll stay high and dry. Just pass it on to the others, Joe, and tell everyone to get back to the ranch before the storm hits. Tell them it's an order.''

''Well, you're the boss, Jake, but it would suit me just fine to check Shell Canyon with you.''

''Thanks, Joe, but I would rest easier if I knew everyone was safe and sound. If I'm not back by…say, ten in the morning…bring a couple of men to the canyon. We'll herd the horses home then. That's it for now. Over and out.''

''Over and out,'' Joe repeated, and their connection was broken.

Jake was riding on soft ground, and the unmistakable hoof prints in the dirt were a snap to follow. This was the clearest trail the stallion had ever left, but Jake couldn't be too elated over finally getting close to him and the mares when there were occasional drops of blood in the dun-colored sandy soil. He'd been hit, all right, and Jake still didn't know which of his men had pulled the trigger. He had confronted them all last night, and no one had stepped forth and owned up to it, probably because Jake had been so enraged he hadn't been very nice about it. In retrospect, he understood that his reaction to the shooting was much different than the shooter must have expected. So, as angry as Jake had been when questioning the crew, it was only natural for the guilty party to think he'd be kicked off the ranch if he admitted his crime.

Checking the men's rifles to see if they'd been fired recently wouldn't prove anything, either, because throughout yesterday Jake had heard several distant shots. One man had shot a rattlesnake, for one thing, and for another, the crew used rifle shots to signal each other when they were out of radio range.

Truth was, and Jake knew it, he might never find out who

had shot the stallion. Unless the man talked about it himself, either in boast or chagrin, it could forever remain a mystery.

Riding along by himself, noticing the increasing wind with one part of his brain and watching the ground with another, Jake used yet a third part to think about last night and Carly, which both thrilled and worried him. Being in love—deeply in love—and having the kind of memories of lovemaking that he had today, would thrill any man.

But there was no getting around the fact that the woman he loved was his boss's daughter. In a lot of cases that scenario wasn't a problem. Jake remembered guys who'd wed the boss's daughter with the boss's blessing.

But Stuart Paxton wasn't just any boss. He was wealthy beyond anything Jake could imagine, and he was a widower who had doted on his one and only child since her birth. Try as he might, Jake could not get past one question: Had Stu ever given him any reason to think that one of his employees might be good enough for his most precious possession?

"Nope," Jake said under his breath. Even though Stuart had always treated him as an equal, he was so far from being Stuart Paxton's equal it would be funny if it wasn't so tragic. They'd started out as equals. As young men they'd been just about as equal as two people could be. But Jake had wasted too many years, and Stuart hadn't wasted even a minute.

Some men were such damned fools, Jake thought in self-disgust.

But would he have ever known that about himself if he hadn't met and fallen in love with Carly?

Feeling down in the mouth, Jake hunched his shoulders against the wind and walked his horse toward the narrow, brushy entrance to Shell Canyon. He would probably never have a real chance with Carly—not anything permanent, at any rate—but he could do one thing for her that she would appreciate and never forget. He could bring in that stallion, hire the best vet in the area to tend his wound, and then let Carly make the decision about what should be done with the wild horse. Jake had the feeling that she wouldn't vote for castration, and that could be the right decision. He would know more about that when he saw the stallion up close.

But whatever she said, he would abide by it. He could, at least, give her that.

The radio on Carly's bed suddenly started speaking! Wondering how she could have forgotten the radio, Carly grabbed it up to listen. There was a lot of static and the sound faded in and out, but she heard a man's voice—unfamiliar—and caught some of his words.

"Jake....Shell Canyon...stallion...orders...Jake said...no, dammit, follow his orders...I'm on my way...you'd better do as he said...pass it on...over and out."

Carly's pulse picked up speed. That broken message sounded to her as though Jake and his men were following the stallion to a place called Shell Canyon. Where on earth was Shell Canyon? *It's probably the place where they plan to finish off the stallion, damn them!*

Sitting on the edge of her bed, she impatiently but cautiously pulled her riding boot onto her left foot. Her ankle certainly wasn't completely healed, but the sprain hadn't been nearly as bad as everyone had thought. It hurt to pull on the boot, but once in place, it provided support and her ankle felt much better. Standing, Carly tried walking and winced only slightly.

"It'll do," she said determinedly. She was not going to baby herself over a piddly little ache in her ankle when Jake and his men were on their way to finish off that stallion!

Leaving her bed unmade again, and remembering that she'd also left Jake's bed in an awful mess, she muttered, "To hell with it," and started down the stairs, carrying the radio. Holding tightly on to the railing with her free hand, she took each step slowly, which added to the impatience gnawing at her. It seemed to take forever, but she was finally on the first floor.

Then, while stowing food into her knapsack, she pushed the radio's talk button and said, "Barney? Are you there? Can you hear me?"

"I hear you, ma'am. Are you okay? Are you ready for breakfast? Jake said to let you sleep, which is the reason I didn't bother you. How's your ankle this morning?"

"Barney, where is Shell Canyon?"

"Shell Canyon, did you say?"

"Yes. Where is it?"

"Well, it's about seven miles southeast of the old mine, and that's about…"

"Never mind. I know where the old mine is. Unless there's more than one old mine. Is there?"

"Oh, sure, there's a whole bunch of old digs in the mountains, but I was talking about the old mine where you sprained your ankle yesterday."

"Good. Great. I know where that is. And Shell Canyon is about seven miles southeast of that, you said?" With one hand Carly shoved packages of fruit, bread and cheese into the knapsack.

"Are you ready for some breakfast now?" Barney asked. "How about some nice blueberry pancakes?"

It dawned on Carly that Barney thought she was still lying in bed, still acting like an invalid and expecting to be waited on.

"Thanks, Barney, but I'm eating as we speak. I'm downstairs in the kitchen."

"You're that much better? Well, for heaven's sake. Who'd a thought it last night?"

"You're right. Who'd a thought it last night?" Carly shook her head. The way she'd behaved in bed with Jake last night, no one would ever believe there was a single thing wrong with her. Not physically anyhow. Mentally, they might think she was a bit off, but certainly not physically. And just what was Jake thinking about that shocking episode today? If he thought she'd been only pretending to be asleep, and maybe chuckling over it, she would brain him.

But that was a whole other problem. She could worry about Jake's take on her behavior last night some other time. Right now, she had to get herself on a horse and make tracks for Shell Canyon. That stallion's life depended on her showing up in time, she was sure of it.

"Barney, just so you won't have reason to worry later on, I'm going to Shell Canyon. You said it's southeast from the old mine. Are we talking about a straight line, or are there landmarks I should watch for? And one other thing. Are any of the men around? I'm doing well with my ankle but I'm a little concerned about saddling a horse."

"Hell's bells," Barney muttered, obviously upset with her. "There's a big storm movin' in. Haven't you noticed the wind? You shouldn't be going anywhere, ma'am."

"I'm going, Barney, storm or no storm. Is there anyone around to saddle my horse?"

"Me," Barney said grudgingly. "I'll go and do it now. Any horse in particular?"

"The gray gelding I've been riding, please. And thank you, Barney. Just leave him at the big corral. I'll be leaving the house as soon as I get everything together. You didn't answer my question about the seven-mile ride between the mine and the canyon. Help me out, Barney. What should I expect?"

"Carly, what you're planning on doing just ain't smart!" There was a pause, then Carly heard Barney sigh. "Okay, I can see you're bent on doing this. The route is pretty direct. Do you have a compass?"

"No. Do you have one I could use, Barney?" It was the first time Barney had used her first name, and his concern touched Carly. "I know you think I'm rash, but this is something I have to do, Barney," she said gently. "If you have a compass I could borrow, just leave it with the horse. Thank you, Barney. Over and out."

Fifteen minutes later Carly left with her knapsack, the radio, the canteen of water and a warm, wind-breaking jacket. She was almost to the big corral when the telephone rang in the house, too far away for her to hear it. After four rings the answering machine switched on, and Jake's recorded voice said, "You've reached Wild Horse Ranch. Leave a message and I'll return your call first chance I get."

Stuart Paxton said, "Jake, hello. And Carly, how are you doing, honey? Okay, here's my message. I'm coming to the ranch tomorrow. Don't worry about my arrival time, but if everything goes as it should, I'll be there about noon, or shortly after. I'm looking forward to seeing you both. Bye for now."

At the corral Carly smiled when she saw the compass tied to the saddle horn. Barney simply couldn't help being a sweet man, she thought as she secured her canteen and knapsack, then gingerly put her left foot in the stirrup and pulled herself up into the saddle. Her reward for so much daring and courage was a sharp, shooting pain in her ankle that made her grit her teeth. But mounting on the left side of a horse was the only way she knew how to do it, and it was over with. She was finally on her way.

Nudging the gray with her knees, she clucked her tongue and got him moving.

The sky was getting darker, more ominous looking. Jake had climbed one of the rocky ledges to check out the canyon, and the wind tore at his clothes and hair. He'd left his hat behind with his horse, because the wind was too strong for a hat. Scanning the canyon with the binoculars he'd brought with him, he spotted the stallion and mares at the far end. They seemed calm enough, huddled together with their hind quarters to the wind. Jake turned the binoculars directly on the stallion.

"You are a beauty, no question about it," he said under his breath, and then frowned when he couldn't see any sign of a wound on the fabulous animal. "Okay, my friend, turn around and let me get a look at your other side." It took a while, but the grazing stallion finally turned enough for Jake to see the wound. It was a seeping furrow on his right rump, a flesh wound, not pretty to look at but not fatal, either. Unless infection set in, of course. That was really the only danger the stallion was in. He was not going to suddenly fall to his knees and die because of that gunshot wound, which was relieving enough for Jake to get a little weak in his own knees. The vet would administer some antibiotics, perhaps clean up the wound a little, and the stallion would be good as new.

Jake moved the binoculars from mare to mare and found them all to be in good shape, too. Lowering the binoculars he studied the canyon mouth and considered various methods of getting that little herd to the ranch. Whatever he decided to do, he couldn't do it in this wind, and it would be much easier with the help of a couple of the men. He would wait until morning.

Climbing back down from the ledge, Jake came to a cave about halfway to the ground. He checked it out, found it to be dry, wind-free and without any signs that animals used it, and decided it would do for the night. It was also near the canyon's entrance, so if the stallion took a notion to move the mares again—not likely in such high wind, but not impossible, either—he would hear them.

Going outside again, he fought the fierce wind to carry his things and several armloads of dried chunks of wood for a fire up to the cave and then to find cover for his horse. He searched the nooks and crannies of the canyon's rock formations and finally found a spot out of the wind with good grazing grass. After leading the horse to the place, Jake used his hat to haul water from a trickling little waterfall to his horse for a drink. Deciding he'd done all he could till the storm passed, Jake climbed back up to his cave.

Standing in the entrance, he saw the first jagged streaks of lightning and heard the ensuing rolls of thunder. It wasn't an unpleasant or disturbing situation for Jake. He'd always liked camping out, and however bad the storm got, he would be dry, safe and comfortable in the cave.

The area's main source of ground moisture was winter snowfalls. Summer storms were totally unpredictable. This one, for instance, could bluster and blow for several hours, then pass on over without raining a drop. Jake wished it *would* rain. The earth could use a good drenching, and he loved how clean and fresh everything smelled after a rainfall.

He stopped watching the lightning to pick up rocks, which he brought inside the cave and used to create a firepit. Going outside for a few more rocks, he caught the barest glimpse of movement just beyond the canyon's entrance. He stopped in his tracks to squint at the spot, wondering what it was that he'd seen. Not that everything movable wasn't moving. Trees were either swaying or bent over from the wind, and ground debris was flying everywhere.

But what he'd glimpsed was something different. Was it a horse?

In seconds he saw very clearly what it was—a horse and a rider. A gray horse and a rider with long, dark, wind-tossed hair. It was Carly!

Jake was suddenly steaming. What was that fool woman doing out here in this kind of windstorm? And the lightning was getting worse by the minute.

He could tell she was calling his name though the sound was swallowed by the wind, but it was proof that she knew he was out there. Wondering which of his men was stupid enough to tell her where he was, Jake angrily watched Carly direct her horse through the entrance of the canyon, then pull him to a stop to look around.

Why was she out here? What in hell did she think *he* was doing out here? And what about her ankle? It couldn't possibly have healed overnight.

"You are the most stubborn, irritating and have-it-your-way woman in the whole damned world,'' Jake muttered. Something gave way in his system and his anger collapsed completely. Carly might be stubborn and strong-willed—and spoiled rotten by her father—but Jake didn't even try to deny his feelings for her. He loved her, always would and that was that.

''Carly!'' he shouted into the wind, and when she began looking for a person to put with the voice she'd heard, he shouted her name again, adding this time, ''Up here! Look up to your right!''

She spotted him. ''What're you doing up there?''

''Tell you later. You wait there,'' Jake shouted. ''I'll come down.''

She wasn't sure she should agree to anything he suggested. Had he and his men found the wounded stallion? Had she gotten here too late to prevent the execution?

Jake didn't wait for an answer from her, but instead ran back into the cave for his jacket and then scrambled down the rocky ledges to the ground. Striding toward Carly, he admired the glory of her long hair blowing in the wind. She was truly a beautiful woman, and his mind suddenly rushed forward to what kind of night they could have in that pleasant little cave. They were alone out here, even more alone than they were in the ranch house.

He realized that he was riding an incredible high right now—due strictly to Carly's presence—so it was quite a shock to see a cold, forbidding look on her face when he approached her.

''Uh, let me, uh, help you down,'' he said without a whole lot of confidence. If she was angry with him about something—hard to believe after last night—then why was she here? She hadn't taken that long ride in gale-force winds just to give him hell, had she?

''I don't see anyone else,'' Carly shouted to be heard over the wind. ''Where's the crew?''

''Would you mind if we talked later?'' Jake shouted back.

He felt the first sprinkles of rain and looked at the sky. "Come on. Let me help you down. I've got my things in a cave. We'll be dry and warm during the storm."

Carly had honestly expected to see the whole crew at Shell Canyon, and it puzzled her that she didn't. But the storm was worsening by the minute, and even though the mere thought of entering a cave scared her, so did fending for herself any longer. She was relieved to have found Jake, for that matter, as she'd been getting pretty worried about finding Shell Canyon, even with a compass.

Letting go of the reins, she laid her hands on Jake's shoulders and let him take her down from the horse. Putting her weight onto her ankle delivered a jolt of pain that had her gritting her teeth, but she didn't let on. If Jake knew she was in pain, he would, at the very least, deliver her a lecture, and she wasn't in the mood to hear a lecture from anyone, least of all a man who would order his men to shoot a horse just because the animal was a bit of a nuisance.

"I want you to wait right here," Jake told her. "I'm going to put your horse with mine, then I'll take you to the cave." He looked into her eyes, hoping to find even a modicum of warmth, some little clue that would tell him she wasn't angry with him at all but had braved the elements just to be with him. He saw nothing consoling, and his heart sank. "I'll be right back," he said tersely.

The second he'd taken the horse, Carly leaned against a huge boulder. Her ankle was throbbing, and the wind was so fierce it was frightening. Not only that, she could feel tiny drops of rain. Any minute now it could start pouring.

She shouldn't have come. She was just too impulsive...and foolhardy. The stallion must be dead or the men would still be here. She couldn't figure out why Jake was hanging around, but maybe it had something to do with the mares.

But no, wouldn't the men have driven the mares back to the ranch when they went? It was no comfort at all to remember that she'd not seen a soul during her ride to the canyon, because there was probably a dozen different ways to get from there to here, or vice versa.

And just where was that cave Jake had mentioned? Lord, if she could just take off her boots and lie down for a while. Her ankle was killing her, feeling even worse now than it had yesterday. She should have stayed in bed today and kept it iced. Wouldn't it be a final straw if she'd done some permanent damage to her poor ankle by chasing after Jake and that stallion?

Dear God, why hadn't she just stayed in New York where she belonged? she thought wearily.

Twelve

Jake came back, leaning into the wind and carrying Carly's knapsack and canteen. "Come on," he said at once. "This weather is going to get a lot worse before it gets better. Let's head for cover."

Carly was afraid of releasing her death grip on the tree, but either she had to make it to Jake's cave under her own power or admit that she'd acted in haste that morning and should be home in bed rather than in the middle of nowhere in what was developing into a major storm.

"Fine," she said in a tone of voice that revealed none of the things she'd been thinking. For instance, she knew now that her ankle was going to hurt like the devil when she walked on that foot, and she didn't want Jake catching on and haranguing her about it. It was simply a matter of looking calm and in control, she told herself, and took a big breath and a step away from the tree.

Jake had already started walking toward the rocky wall of the canyon and didn't see Carly's wince. Grateful that his back was to her and that he was concentrating on bucking the wind, she tried hard to walk without putting her full weight on her left foot. She wasn't doing too bad with keeping up, but then she saw the rocky face of the canyon wall and frowned severely while attempting to spot a cave. Surely it was at ground level!

Jake stopped and turned to face her. "There's a good trail. I've been up and down it a dozen times. Stay close behind me."

"Surely you jest," she said weakly. "You're not really expecting me to maneuver myself up that sheer cliff."

"It's not so sheer, and the cave is not that far up there." Jake peered at her suspiciously. There was the tiniest note of something not quite right in her voice. Not alarm, not fear, but something off-key. "What's wrong? Are you afraid of heights?"

"Of course not," she snapped churlishly. Blaming Jake for every discomfort, worry and irritation she'd suffered since coming to Wyoming only seemed logical. *For God's sake, who else would I blame?*

She was suddenly furious again. "Lead the way," she all but shrieked in his face, just to be heard above the howling wind.

Jake frowned. "What're you mad about now?" he shouted.

"You could try the patience of a saint! Just go, would you? I'm tired of fighting the wind!"

Jake shook his head in disgust. How could he love such a temperamental woman? Carly could be sweet as pie or tart as a lemon. Right now she looked as though she would like to tar and feather him, as though he was the cause of her being caught in a storm and seeking cover in a cave. Turning away from her, he began the ascent up the crude, rocky trail.

Carly took a big breath. It was now or never. Somehow she had to follow him to the cave. What was a little pain, anyhow? she asked herself. She had endured worse physical pain before, heaven knew, and some of the mental anguish she'd lived through during her marriage had far surpassed the discomfort of a sprained ankle.

Jake scrambled up the trail as surefooted as a mountain goat, unworried that Carly wouldn't be right behind him. At the mouth of the cave he looked back and felt like a jerk. She was gingerly—very gingerly—picking her way through the rocks. Obviously, her bad ankle was a serious hindrance. She was probably hurting like hell and too damned prideful to say so.

"Okay," he muttered. "Enough is enough." Dropping her knapsack and canteen, he went back down the trail.

She was concentrating so hard on what she was doing that she didn't see him until he was standing right in front of her.

"What?" she shouted belligerently. The wind took that one word, completely depleted its strength and made Carly sound as though she were a mile away.

"Your ankle is hurting, isn't it?" Jake shouted back.

"Only a little," she replied, resentful that she would have to admit even that much to him. "Don't worry about it. I'm doing fine."

"Like hell you are. I'm going to carry you the rest of the way. Just relax and let me do the work, okay?"

"No way!"

Jake ignored her objection, bent over and pulled her forward over his left shoulder. "Dammit, stop wiggling," he told her.

"Then put me down! I am not a sack of potatoes, you...you cretin!"

"Believe me, I know you're not a sack of potatoes." Chuckling, Jake patted her nicely rounded fanny.

Her head was just above the hem of the back of his jacket, and her arms were dangling in midair. She felt like an idiot, being shuttled along *exactly* the way a man would carry a sack of potatoes, regardless of his comment to the contrary.

As for him patting her fanny, how dare he take advantage of this indignity?

Then she realized how precarious was her perch. Looking down was terrifying. Feeling a bit nauseous, she shut her eyes and prayed for solid ground. If Jake should trip over something, or even stumble, they could both be killed.

"Good girl," Jake said when he realized that she wasn't moving a finger. Obviously, she had accepted his intervention, which was only sensible, but who knew better than he that Carly was often more impulsive than sensible.

Whatever Carly's personality, though, or however she reacted to events and people, Jake knew he had it bad for her. And whether she would ever talk about it, or admit to anything, she had to have some feelings for him, too. Those feelings might be nothing more than a potent physical attraction for him, but raging hormones were pretty darned hard to ignore.

Finally reaching the cave, he entered it, walked around the rocky outcropping protecting the interior from the elements and said quietly, "I'm going to set you over there on that rock for now."

The silence of the cave after the broiling melee outside was startling to Carly. She opened her eyes, registered the gray, shadowy interior of the cave, and then felt Jake gently lower her feet to the sandy floor and finally help her sit on a good-sized rock.

"I know it seems dark in here," Jake said. "But a fire will change everything. Are you all right sitting there?"

"I'm fine." Warily she looked around the cave. "Are you sure this isn't some animal's den?"

"Positive." Jake went outside and brought in Carly's knapsack and canteen. He put her things with his, then set to work on building a fire.

Carly remained silent for a while, but it was so deathly quiet in the cave that she needed to hear a voice, if only her own.

"Have…have you used this cave before?"

"No, this is the first time for this one." Jake lit a match and put the flame to his tinder. It ignited and he proceeded to fan his blaze and add fuel until the fire was burning exactly as he wanted it to.

"That's nice," Carly said quietly. The firelight was casting images on the walls of the cave, and the air was quickly warming up.

Jake left the fire and approached her. "Carly, I think we should get that boot off your foot."

There was no longer any point to Carly acting as though everything was peachy when he knew it wasn't, so she spoke honestly. "It will swell again."

"I'm sure it will, but we're here for the night and you're going to have to give your ankle some relief."

She was visibly taken aback. "We're here for the night? Why? Is the storm that bad?" Then some previous thoughts caught up with her. "Why are we here at all, Jake? Why are you here without the men? And maybe I should ask the biggest question of all." She hesitated slightly, afraid of how Jake might answer the "biggest" question but driven to hear it. Lifting her chin she looked him in the eyes and said, "Is the stallion dead?"

"Is that what you think? Is that the reason you risked further injury to your ankle by riding clear out here?"

"Frankly, yes," she said coolly. "And your being alone out here appears pretty damning, because if the stallion was still at large you'd still have the crew chasing him."

"Oh, really. Fat lot you know about it." Jake narrowed his eyes on her. "But you think you know, don't you? You judged me as a horse killer the second you got off that helicopter, and if you lived on this ranch for thirty years and so did that stallion, you would stand by that judgment every minute of every day. Well, let me tell you something…"

"Just hold it right there! I judged you? Suppose you back up and recall our conversation about the stallion the day I

got here. I asked what you would do with him when you
captured him, and you, you rude, inhospitable phony, you
said that someone, either you or some of your men, intended
to shoot him. I became understandably upset, and since
then..."

Jake cut in. "I happen to remember that conversation, apparently a little better than you do. What I told you was that
some of the men suggested shooting the stallion, and when
you got all blustery and out of shape over that idea, I explained that I had no intentions of shooting any animal, least
of all a horse."

Carly's jaw dropped. "You did not!"

"Did so."

"Damn you, you never said anything of the kind! In fact,
you were so annoyed because I even wanted to discuss the
stallion that you were curt and unpleasant, and...and..."

"You didn't just want to discuss the stallion, you *insisted*
on it."

"So? What was wrong with that? If you'd care to remember I had just seen him from the air and I was incredibly
impressed." After a brief pause she said, "I guess I couldn't
believe that anyone would even consider killing something
so beautiful. You were...a terrible disappointment. Dad had
always spoken so highly of you, and practically the first
words out of your mouth after we met were about the de-
struction of a magnificent horse."

Jake knelt down in front of her. "Am I still a disappointment?"

She searched the dark depths of his fabulous blue eyes,
and a thrill went up her spine. He was an incredible lover,
and every moment spent in his arms was suddenly upon her,
weakening resolve, resentment and certainly eradicating any
remnants of disappointment.

And yet she couldn't give him everything. Love wreaked
havoc with one's emotions, causing the highest highs and the
lowest lows. There were moments when she could think to

herself about having fallen in love with Jake, but letting him know her true feelings was another matter entirely.

And so she said, rather flippantly, "You don't disappoint me in bed."

His eyes became even darker. Was she trying to hurt him? And if she was, was it because of that damned stallion? He'd been on the verge of helping her over to the mouth of the cave, handing her the binoculars and telling her where to look so she could see the stallion for herself. But for her to actually say to his face that he was a terrible disappointment hurt too much for him to immediately get over it.

"Well," he drawled lazily, concealing the pain in his heart with a casual and flirty grin, "it's going to be a long night. Since I don't disappoint you in bed, that's where we'll spend our time." Taking her left foot in his hands, he brought it to his lap.

"Uh, Jake, I didn't mean..."

"I know exactly what you meant, baby. It was great for me, too. Believe me, you haven't disappointed me in bed, either. Okay, I'm going to slowly work off your boot. Try not to help."

Carly felt like bawling. She hadn't expressed herself at all well. She could have let him know he'd disappointed her with the stallion without bringing sex into the conversation. Now he thought she'd been hinting for more of the same and was going to do his best to provide her with one very hot night.

Oh, that idea had some appeal, make no mistake. But each time she made love with Jake Banyon brought her that much closer to some heavy-duty heartache.

I'm in over my head with Jake, that's the problem. He's forever one step ahead of me, and it doesn't bother him at all to use any situation to his own advantage. He might be a great ranch manager—if Dad is right about that—but he's unscrupulous with women, and I fell for his macho charisma hook, line and sinker. And now I'm stuck here in this little

*cave with him until he decides to leave. God help me, am I
ever going to do anything right?*

"There, that does it." Jake set her boot aside and using
just the pads of his fingertips very gently examined her foot
through her stocking. "It's a little swollen. Not too bad,
though. How does it feel without the boot?"

"Better. Jake, I...I think I gave you the wrong idea
about...about..."

"About you and me?" He spoke with complete nonchalance, as though the subject wasn't burning a hole in his gut
at all but rather was really too trivial to concern either of
them. He grinned a deliberately devilish, lustful grin.
"Honey, you said it plain as day. We're great in bed. Hey,
how about last night? There you were, waiting for me to get
home, all warm and silky sweet just for me. Something like
that really lifts a man's spirit. But you already knew that or
you wouldn't have done it, right?"

"Jake...it wasn't, uh...I mean, I didn't..."

"Honey, it was and you did. Several times, if I remember
right."

Carly's face flamed. "You are deliberately misconstruing
my words!"

"Weren't you talking about last night?" Jake asked innocently.

"Uh...yes...but..."

"Thought so." Patting her calf, Jake got to his feet. "You
just sit right there and I'll take care of the fire and then put
together some supper for us." Whistling between his teeth,
he laid some wood on the fire and then picked up her knapsack. "Do you have any food in this?"

"Yes. Help yourself." She knew she sounded like a petulant child, but how dare he presume so much? She had not
come out here for an all-night orgy, for heaven's sake. Was
sex all he ever thought about? Well, it wasn't all she thought
about, and, in fact, Jake just might be using that subject to
avoid talking about her real reason for being here.

"What about the stallion?" she demanded.

Jake sent her a friendly little glance. "What about him?"

Carly could feel her body tense up. "Is he dead?"

"I don't think so, but…" Jake shrugged dramatically. "He *was* shot yesterday, you know."

"Of course I know he was shot," Carly snapped. "And you gave the order. What I'd like to know now is why you're here."

"Didn't you run into any of the men on your way out here?"

"I saw no one, not a soul. Why? Was the crew riding back to the ranch at the same time that I was riding to this canyon?"

"Could be." Jake had opened and spread out his sleeping bag, and was now setting out the food in Carly's knapsack and what he'd brought with him.

"It could be? What kind of answer is that? Dammit, was the crew on their way in while I was riding away from the ranch or not?"

"What difference does it make. You're here and they're there." Jake sent her a completely sensual look. "Which makes things really sweet for us, babe. A whole night together? No one around? Oh, yeah, it's going to be one for the books."

Carly reached for her boot. "That does it! I've had just about all of that kind of innuendo I can stomach for one day."

Jake stood up. "What're you doing?"

"I'm leaving. What does it look like I'm doing?" She tried to pull on her boot and nearly blacked out from the pain in her foot. "Ohhh," she groaned.

Jake rushed over and took the boot from her hand. Without a by-your-leave or anything else, he scooped her up from the rock and growled, "Put your arms around my neck and hang on. I'm going to show you something."

More than five feet off the ground and in his arms again,

Carly felt horribly vulnerable. She did her best to look fierce, though. "Put me down, you damned bully!"

"In a minute." Jake strode around the outcropping of rock that blocked the mouth of the cave and, instantly, the storm was upon them. "Now," he said gruffly. "Are you sure you want to go out in that? It's raining so hard I doubt you could see your hand in front of your own face. You'd be lost twenty feet away from the canyon."

"I have a compass," Carly said resentfully. "And I know how to use it."

Jake thought a second, then turned and carried her back to her rock. He lowered her gently, then walked away. "Fine. If you want to leave, go ahead and leave."

Carly felt completely trapped. Outside was one of the worst storms she'd ever seen and inside was Jake, lying in wait for her like a spider after a fly. Maybe she'd brought this on herself, but she certainly hadn't expected to find Jake holed up in an intimate little cave. In truth, she'd expected to see the whole crew in Shell Canyon. Why had the men gone back to the ranch and Jake stayed behind?

She was getting fed up with Jake's evasive answers to her questions and she vowed on the spot that no matter how cute he tried to be about last night and what a great time they could have tonight, he was getting nothing from her but attitude, because that was all he deserved.

Realizing that she was hungry and the food that Jake was setting out looked good, she rose from her rock, limped over to the sleeping bag and sat down.

Jake glanced over to her. "I take it you're not leaving?"

"Maybe I am, maybe I'm not," she retorted. "Right now I'm going to eat something. I might decide to leave later on, I might not. Figure it out for yourself. That's the sort of answer you've given me every time I've asked you something, so don't expect anything different from me."

"Apparently it's revenge time," Jake said dryly.

"Think what you want. I personally don't give a damn."

"Does this mean we won't be sharing the sleeping bag tonight?"

"Oh, shut up and hand me some of that cheese!"

Every time Carly hobbled over to the cave's entrance, the storm looked worse. She learned how really bad it was when nature called and she had to go outside for privacy. Jake saw her taking his flashlight and offered to go with her.

"Like I want you with me?" she said sarcastically. "When you have to go outside for personal reasons, do you want me holding the flashlight for you?"

"Of course not."

Shooting him a look that said it all, Carly limped away for her jacket.

When she came back she was wet and cold, and she sat close to the fire to get warm again. Along with heat, the fire provided light, and the little cave was cozy as a nest.

Jake poked at the fire with a long stick and asked, "How's the foot?"

Since she was still determined to avoid a straightforward answer to any question he might ask, she sniffed and said, "Why on earth would you care?"

Jake stared broodingly into the dancing flames, and for a long time neither of them said anything.

Finally Jake said, "It's getting late. You can use the sleeping bag."

"Hmph," she snorted. "It's your bag, you use it."

"And you'll do what all night, sleep on the bare ground?"

"I...I'll keep the fire going. I'm not sleepy anyway."

"Oh, so you'll sit up all night. I don't think so." Getting up, he started preparing the sleeping bag.

Carly squared her shoulders indignantly. "If you're fixing that for me, you're wasting your time. Let me ask you something. Exactly what is there about me that makes you think you can order me around? Do I look like an automaton? A witless child? Or maybe it isn't me at all. Maybe it's you.

Maybe you've issued orders to everyone around you all your life.''

"Yeah, right," Jake said dryly. He stopped smoothing the sleeping bag to look at her. "You know, for an intelligent person you come up with some pretty screwy ideas."

"Screwy or accurate?" she said with stinging sarcasm. "You're the kind of man who would accuse a woman of a mental deficiency rather than let her really get to know you."

"And I suppose you're an open book? Don't sit there and act as though you've encouraged any genuine closeness between us, Carly. In bed we connect. Out of bed we don't. Maybe I haven't told you anything about myself, but I'm no more closemouthed about the past than you are."

"I didn't encourage sex between us, either, but that didn't stop you!"

"Oh, so everything was my fault? My doing? I'll admit I shouldn't have made that first pass, but what about last night? You were in my bed stark naked."

"Only to use your damned phone! God, the ego of some men." Carly rolled her eyes.

Jake sat down with a thud. "You were in my room to use the phone? Why didn't you say so?"

"Because I was sleeping!" she shouted. He looked at her until she felt as though his eyes were boring holes into her. "What?" she said in a demanding tone. "I suppose you don't believe me."

"Uh, if you slept through the whole thing, how do you remember it so well?"

Carly felt her face get pink. "I...I suppose I wasn't asleep the...the whole time."

"Exactly when did you wake up?" Jake asked softly. "Was it when I first held your naked body against mine, or could it have been much later on when you were crying out and digging your nails into my back?"

"Do you have to be so crude?"

"Do you have to be such a liar? You might have been

asleep when I got under that blanket with you, and you might have remained drowsy during the foreplay...extremely memorable, by the way...but you're kidding yourself and lying to me with that 'I was sleeping' excuse. What I'd like to know is why you think you need an excuse—more like an apology, to be honest—for making love.''

''There are a few things about you that I'd like to know, too, and since I'm positive you have no intention of telling me anything, just forget your questions about me, Banyon!''

''What do you want to know?''

She blinked at him across the fire. ''What are you talking about?''

''I merely asked what you'd like to know about me.''

''And I suppose you're just going to roll over and talk your head off,'' she said with exaggerated sweetness.

''Yes. And God knows when I'll feel this way again, so if you've got questions you'd like some answers for, you'd better ask them now.''

Was he serious? Carly's pulse rate increased. Would he really talk about himself? Oh, yes, she would love to pick his brain. There was an aura of mystery about Jake that she'd never run into before, and to say it was intriguing was an understatement. He was intriguing, and so sexy and handsome in that firelight she began thinking of all they had done in his bed last night.

Feeling overheated and achy in intimate spots of her body, she took off her jacket and smiled weakly. ''It...it's getting a little too warm in here.''

Jake's grin was lopsided, very male and very knowing. ''Yeah, it is.'' Turning back to the sleeping bag, he unzipped it again and smoothed it open next to the fire. Then he got up and walked around the fire to Carly. He held out his hand to her. ''It's time to lie down and rest. We'll stay dressed and use our jackets for blankets. And we'll talk. I promise. Give me your hand so I can help you get up.''

Carly looked at his hand and felt the breath catch in her

throat. And then, slowly and hesitantly, she brought up her hand and laid it in his.

She was, so it seemed, unable to say no to Jake.

The worst part of that supposition was that even though it scared her, it also thrilled her.

In truth, nothing else in all of her life had ever thrilled her so much.

Thirteen

On her back, using her rolled-up jacket as a pillow, Carly watched the moving reflections of the fire on the ceiling of the cave. It wasn't the dark old hole in the ground she'd thought of when Jake had first mentioned the word *cave*, rather it was hewn from some sort of pale, cream-colored, sandy-looking rock that reflected the firelight beautifully.

Jake was next to her, also on his back, but there was at least a foot of space between them. "I'll watch the fire through the night," he said quietly.

"It needs wood every hour. You're going to wake up once an hour all night?"

"I've done it before. It's no big deal."

It was amazing to Carly that they were the same two people who had made such wild, passionate love last night, because tonight they talked without looking at each other, and kept strictly to their own side of the sleeping bag.

"You must have an internal alarm clock if you can do that," she murmured.

"Guess so." After a moment of silence, he asked, "Are you comfortable enough? How's your ankle?"

"It's all right, and so am I."

"Good. Are you tired now, or do you still want to ask questions about my past?"

"You said I'm no open book, either, Jake. Do you want to ask questions?"

"I do if you do."

Carly sighed impatiently. "Okay, forget it." She really didn't feel like playing any more evasive games with Jake. He could take his secrets—if secrets were what he was guarding so diligently—to the grave.

And she could take hers back to New York when she went home. A great melancholy suddenly seized Carly, and she sighed again. She couldn't languish in Wyoming forever, although what she would be rushing back to in New York escaped her. It was home, of course, but that was all it was. There was no job awaiting her, very few friends, and probably worst of all, she had not one single exciting idea about what to do with the rest of her life. Actually, now that she thought about it, she was more contented living at Wild Horse Ranch than she'd been anywhere else in years, even with Jake as a disturbing distraction. In fact, the prospect of leaving the ranch and going home was surprisingly discomfiting. Was that because of Jake, or would she be feeling the same way if some old geezer had been managing the ranch and she'd never met Jake Banyon?

While Carly lay silent and thinking, so did Jake. The difference in their expressions was that he wore a serious frown as his mind jumped around. He and Carly could become very close tonight, and while he wasn't sure that was the wisest course for the two of them to take, he also wasn't sure anymore that he would choose his job over Carly, if it came down to that.

"No, let's not forget it," he said quietly. "How about if

we take turns. I'll ask you a question, which you'll answer honestly, then you will ask one of me. What do you say?''

He had definitely surprised Carly, but he'd also pleased her so much that her mood instantly lightened. Speaking teasingly, she said, ''Sounds okay to me, but why do you get to be first?''

''Because I'm bigger and older than you.''

''Ha-ha, very funny. Well, I suppose it doesn't matter who's first, so go ahead. What would you like to know?''

''When Stu called about you coming to Wyoming, he said something about your having a bad time getting over your marriage and divorce.''

''Dad said that?'' Carly felt the same guilty pang over worrying her dad that she'd lived with for a long time. ''I know I've caused him a lot of headaches and I suppose he had to tell you something about why I would suddenly come to the ranch when I'd avoided it since childhood, but... Oh, well, it's water under the bridge.'' Carly took a breath. ''The truth is that my marriage was a nightmare, and the divorce was a relief.'' After a moment she added, ''An enormous relief.''

''All right, my first question is what made the marriage a nightmare?''

Carly laughed shakily. ''You don't intend to make this easy, do you?''

''Is it too painful to talk about?''

''That's another question.''

''But you didn't answer the first one.''

''No, I guess I didn't,'' she murmured. ''Okay, here's the sordid truth. My ex was...was abusive.''

Jake pushed himself up to an elbow to see her face. ''Physically abusive?''

''All kinds of abusive.'' Carly turned her head so Jake couldn't see her eyes. ''I was pregnant once, Jake, and deliriously happy about it. He wasn't and he couldn't stop letting me know how he felt. I...I had a miscarriage.''

Jake put his hand on her arm. "Carly, I'm so sorry. God, I never expected to hear something like that. No wonder you don't like talking about it."

She brought her head around and found herself looking into his eyes. "I left him, of course. He never showed his face at the hospital, and Dad took me home with him. That was the end, and, as I said before, the divorce was an enormous relief."

"Did you ever really love him?"

"Yes, I really did. Seems impossible now, but there was a time when I loved him madly."

Jake flopped onto his back again, only now he was no more than an inch away from Carly. "You loved him, and he hurt you in a way you will never be able to forget. Love's not all it's cracked up to be, is it?"

"You've got that right. To be honest, I had reached the point of thinking there was no such thing as true love. As for romance, forget it. I had come to believe that the word *romance* was invented by some poet or playwright so he could justify the people he wrote about behaving like idiots."

"I didn't put it in that context but I felt the same way."

"You did?" It occurred to Carly that they were talking in the past tense. *I had reached...I felt...I thought.* What about now? Did she feel differently about romance and love than she had before meeting Jake? "I think it's my turn for a question," she said softly.

"Yeah, you're right."

"Were you, uh, ever married?"

"No."

She hesitated because he'd spoken with such finality, but that answer hadn't even taken the edge off her curiosity.

"Jake, you can't respond to my questions with one-word answers," she murmured. "That's worse than no answer at all."

"I know." Jake took a long breath. "I was two weeks from the ceremony when my fiancée dumped me."

"And you loved her?"

"I was nuts about her." Jake snorted out a cynical laugh. "Let's just say I was nuts, period, and let it go at that."

Carly's heart ached for what he must have gone through. "When did that happen, Jake? How long ago?"

"I was fresh out of high school."

Startled over that time frame, she turned her head to look at him and found her face to be mere inches from his. "I…guess I don't understand," she said in a near whisper. "High school was a long time ago. Was that your only experience with love?"

"You're thinking that kids that age only feel puppy love, Carly, and that's just not true. I was knocked for a loop when she told me it was over, and it took me years to…to get myself back on track."

"Jake," she said softly, "are you back on track?"

He let some time go by before answering. "I'm going to tell you all of it. After she dumped me, nothing else mattered. She was all I could think about, and I made a complete fool of myself following her around until she left town."

"Was the town Tamarack? Is Wyoming your home?"

"No. I grew up on a ranch, but it was in Montana. Carly, look at me." Jake turned to his side to face her, and when she faced him, he took her hand and she let him twine their fingers together. Lying so close and looking into each other's eyes was so intimate that Carly felt tears burning her nose, but she said nothing and waited to hear what Jake had to say.

"I threw it all away, Carly," he said huskily. "My father's respect, my own self-respect and any money I earned. Threw it all away because I felt so damned sorry for myself. This is the part I want you to know. I…I not only drank myself senseless, I picked up any woman who gave me a second glance."

Carly bit her lip. "Do you know what I'm saying?" Jake asked, almost harshly. "I slept with any woman who was willing. Didn't matter what she looked like or if she was married. If she was willing, so was I. For years all I did was work just enough to get a little dough, then drink and chase women till it was gone.''

"You were trying to self-destruct,'' Carly whispered raggedly. "Oh, Jake, why do we do such awful things to ourselves?''

"You haven't done anything that bad to yourself.''

"I didn't turn to whiskey and meaningless sex, no, but neither was I getting over blaming and even despising myself for marrying the wrong man. I guess Dad thought the ranch would be therapeutic, and...and...''

"And it might have been, if it weren't for me.'' Jake let go of her hand to lay his along the side of her face. "I'm sorry, but even now, knowing your sad story and talking about my own, I still want you. Carly, when you stepped off that helicopter, something struck me right between the eyes. It made me angry, because I'd been so sure that I'd made a good life for myself out here. Then, there you were, and all my good intentions turned to dust.''

"Jake, I want you, too,'' she whispered, and she turned her head just a little, just enough to press her lips to his palm. Then she laid her hand on his chest. "I love your body.''

"I love your body,'' he whispered back. "Carly, I...I love you.''

Her heart nearly stopped beating. "Don't say it unless you mean it...please.''

"I mean it. I swear I've never meant anything more in my life.''

"Jake, I hear a *but* in your voice.''

"Carly, the *but* is your dad.''

"Dad!'' she exclaimed. "You certainly don't think he would care if you and I...I mean, if he learned that you and I...''

"Have been having an affair, almost since you got here?'' Jake unzipped her jeans and slipped his hand inside of them, going under her panties and sliding downward until he'd reached his goal.

Looking into his eyes, she opened her legs to give him more room. "If you're in love with me, isn't what we have together...what we're doing right now...more than an affair?"

"It is if you love me too." He began tantalizing her most sensitive spot. "Is there any chance that you might love me, Carly?" he asked almost sadly.

"Right this second I love you like crazy," she panted. "Help me get out of these jeans, Jake. And get rid of yours."

Everything fled Jake's mind but what she wanted. "Is it warm enough in here to take everything off?"

"It's warm enough for me. I'm burning up!"

Naked and zipped into the sleeping bag together, they talked drowsily. "I'll bet Dad sympathized when you told him about your past," Carly murmured.

"I never told him. I've never talked about it before, not with anyone." Jake tenderly kissed her bare shoulder.

"I wish you'd have told Dad." Carly sighed softly. "Sorry, I'm not condemning anything you have or haven't done. It's just that no one could ever find a more compassionate person to unload on."

"Carly, I have the highest regard for your dad. I respect and like him and, in a way, I suppose I envy him."

"Envy him?"

"Look, I grew up on a ranch, he grew up on a ranch. Our lives started out in almost the same exact way. But compare where we're both at now or, better yet, compare where Stu was at my present age."

"You're talking about net worth."

"Isn't that how a man's worth is measured in today's world?"

"I guess, but that's to the world at large. On a personal level, money's not that important."

Jake laughed sharply. "Carly, I'm your dad's hired hand. He pays my salary and probably has a better idea of any potential I might have than I do myself. You had one lousy relationship, do you think if he found out about us he'd be thrilled that you'd set your sights so low again?"

"Jake, my ex-husband was wealthy. His whole family was wealthy. Money doesn't make a person decent and kind and loving. I can't believe that you'd even worry about how Dad might react to hearing about us. He wants me to be happy."

"Are you?"

Everything that had happened since the helicopter ride from Cheyenne to the ranch flashed through Carly's mind. "Almost," she said quietly.

"Almost doesn't cut it, sweetheart. I've lived with *almost,* and so have you. *Almost* isn't good enough."

"I know it isn't."

"So, what's the problem? Or are there too many to name? Don't think I've forgotten that you're a city woman, Carly. Maybe the isolation of the ranch is bothering you. And Tamarack's not much of a town. Then there's…"

"Oh, for goodness sake, stop it! The isolation of the ranch is not bothering me, and I like Tamarack. Actually, the only thing that does bother me about the ranch itself is the house. Why don't you have a housekeeper, and why has Dad let the place get in such bad shape?"

"All of that is my fault, Carly. Stu told me to hire a house-keeper, and I didn't want a woman on the place. Since male housekeepers are pretty scarce in Wyoming, I just put the whole thing out of my mind."

"And let the house go to ruin."

"Do you really think it's ruined?"

"What it is is filthy dirty, Jake," Carly said dryly. "Forget it for now. What I'd like you to do is to think hard and look for a reason why I might not be completely happy."

He fell silent, then he let out a whoop of laughter, which

startled Carly so much that she sat up and glared down at him. "Is something funny?" she demanded.

"Yes and no."

"Oh, now there's a straightforward, clear-cut answer for you," she drawled.

"Stop trying to pick a fight and come here." He pulled her down and settled her into his arms again. Then he put his lips against her cheek and murmured, "You're not happy because of that wild stallion."

"And you find that amusing?"

"Carly, he's not dead. He and the mares are at the far end of the canyon. A couple of the men are coming out here in the morning, and we'll be driving the herd back to the ranch. A vet has already been called. He'll be waiting to examine the stallion's wound."

He realized that she'd gone stiff in his arms. "I thought you'd be pleased," he said.

"I...I'm furious! You let me believe he was dead!"

"I never said that, Carly."

"Maybe not in those exact words, but you let me believe..."

"Carly, we've fought over that horse a dozen times. I never intended to kill him and I'm sorry I didn't say it the day we met. I should have said it again and again and in every imaginable way, so that you couldn't possibly misunderstand."

"You didn't want me at the ranch and so you let me believe the absolute worst. Do you have any idea of how I suffered over horrifying visions in my head of that beautiful horse being gunned down, just because he *is* a horse? A stallion? A male animal whose very nature makes him seek out mates?"

"Sort of like people, huh? Men, women, stallions, mares."

"Well...yes." Carly was beginning to relax. The stallion was alive and safe, and the man she loved was in love with her, too. "This has been...a most unusual trip," she murmured reflectively. "I only came to the ranch because Dad asked me to. He said I might find it peaceful enough to do some serious healing."

"And did you?"

"Well, first there was the stallion to worry about, then there was you, Jake. You really caught me off guard, you know. Dad often talked about you, but he never once hinted that you were young and good-looking. My first look at you made me feel like I'd just stuck a finger into a light socket."

Jake laughed quietly, deep in his throat. "Same darned thing I felt when I first saw you. Guess we're both pretty shocking, huh?"

Carly yawned and snuggled against him. "Shocking enough to be incredibly exciting."

"Do you really think I'm exciting, honey?"

Yawning again, Carly answered drowsily. "Let me sleep for a few minutes, then ask me that again."

Jake smiled and kissed her good-night. He hoped that he would drop off, too, but there was a lot on his mind to keep him awake, things that kept going around and around in his head. For one, Carly wasn't a bit worried about Stuart's re-action to his daughter having a sexual relationship with his ranch manager, but Jake was.

He'd committed himself tonight, Jake realized. He'd said the binding words *I love you,* and he still meant them. With Carly he knew in his soul that he always would mean them, but he and Carly weren't the only players in this little drama. Regardless of Carly's confidence in how her dad would take the news, Jake kept seeing disappointment on Stuart Paxton's face.

If this thing with Carly was going to go on—and Jake couldn't pretend, even to himself, that it wouldn't—then he was going to have to talk to Stuart about it. He owed a lot to Stuart Paxton, and he could not disrespect his employer and friend by sleeping with his daughter and keeping it a secret.

Eventually Jake dozed, and he woke up about an hour later, saw that the fire was almost out and quietly and cautiously slid out of the sleeping bag. Carly sighed in her sleep, and Jake looked at her adoringly for a moment, then poked the embers back to life and added wood to the flickering flames.

Wondering how the weather was doing, Jake walked around the big rocks to the mouth of the cave and looked outside. He was pleasantly surprised. The storm had passed completely, and the canyon was so brightly lighted from a full moon and billions of stars that Jake could see the stallion and mares quite clearly.

"Carly's got to see this," he said under his breath. He went back inside the cave, knelt beside the sleeping bag and gently shook Carly's shoulder. "Honey, wake up. There's something you have to see."

"Hmm, what?"

"Get up...just for a few minutes." Rising to his feet, Jake pulled on his jeans.

Groggy and dull-witted, Carly sat up. "What are we doing?"

Jake picked up his shirt and handed it to her. "Put this on. I have to show you something."

"Jake, I'm tired."

"I know you are, but this is a once-in-a-million sight, honey."

"Oh, all right." Carly pulled on his shirt and then took his hand so he could help her to her feet. She tested the strength of her ankle by putting her weight on her left foot. "It hardly hurts at all," she told Jake.

"Glad to hear it. Okay, what I want you to see is outside. Ready?"

He was so boyishly enthused over whatever it was that he wanted her to see that she couldn't resent him for disturbing her sleep. "I'm ready," she said with a smile.

Jake hugged her. "You're a doll." Then his gaze went up and down her. "A pretty cute doll in that big shirt of mine."

"Wanna do something about it, cowboy?" she challenged teasingly.

"You bet I do, but first things first." He took her hand again and led her outside.

"Oh, my goodness," she exclaimed. "The sky is clear as a bell. Oh, Jake, I've never seen so many stars. It's fabulous."

"Yes, it is, but take a look over there." Jake pointed.

Carly followed the direction of his finger and gasped, "The stallion!"

"And the mares." Jake stood behind her and wrapped his arms around her. "Beautiful, aren't they?" he said softly.

She leaned back against him. "So beautiful they take my breath," she whispered. "Or maybe I'm breathless because of you."

Jake pressed his lips to the delectable curve of her neck and let his hands slide into the front opening of his shirt. There, on that rocky ledge, he caressed her breasts and her belly, running his hands up and down her torso.

"You're so beautiful, Carly," he whispered hoarsely. "Your skin is like satin."

She could feel his arousal pressing into her and knew they would make love again. Dreamily she watched the stallion and mares and savored every sensation Jake was awakening within her.

"You said it before, but I didn't," she whispered. "I love you, Jake."

"I'll say it again. I'll say it a million times. I love you, Carly."

But neither of them said a word about marriage, and the strange part was that each of them was afraid that the other one would.

Carly and Jake were ready and waiting when the men arrived at the canyon the next morning in bright sunlight. Carly noticed some curious expressions—a few raised eyebrows and even a smirk—because she was there with Jake, but she really didn't care what anyone might think of her having spent the night with him. Since she intended to spend every night with him from this day forward, anyone inclined to gossip about it would soon find the relationship old hat.

Driving the stallion and mares to the ranch buildings turned out to be great fun for Carly. She watched the men and how they knew exactly what to do to keep the little herd together and headed in the right direction, and she realized how much she loved this land and ranch life in general. There was no question in her mind about leaving now. She was going to stay there with Jake for as long as he loved her, which she believed wholeheartedly was a lifelong condition.

In truth, she had never been happier. Riding with those men was pure reality, but for Carly it had a fairy-tale quality that made her feel youthful and upbeat and completely carefree.

The ranch compound came into view, and Carly thought of her dad growing up here and then leaving for college and never living here again. Paxton family roots were in this ranch, going back four generations. For the first time she questioned what her father would say when she told him about her and Jake and that she had come to love the ranch almost as much as she did Jake Banyon. Would Stuart understand and accept that his only child had found what he had not on this beautiful land?

"The vet's there," Jake said as he rode his horse up next to Carly's.

"How do you know?"

"That yellow van is his." Jake squinted his eyes to see better. "That's Timothy, the vet, in the red shirt. I can see his heavy black beard. But who's that standing with him? Can you tell?"

Carly tried to make out the second man standing at a corral, but they were still too far away. "No, but he looks vaguely familiar, even from this distance."

"That's what I thought." Jake sent her a glance. "Carly, don't let the men's curiosity about you and me get you down. It'll die out in no time."

She laughed happily. "Jake, my love, there's not a thing in the world that could get me down today."

Laughing himself, Jake nudged his horse into a run and chased down one of the mares who had wandered a little too far from the herd.

Carly drew a long, contented breath. The stallion was surprisingly docile today and still the most beautiful horse she'd ever seen, and Carly passed the time in planning ways to make friends with the wild horse. Now, of course, she could ask questions of any man on the place, Jake included.

Everything felt so right, in fact, that Carly couldn't stop smiling. She watched Jake and felt her heart swell with love. He was so incredibly handsome—a sensual, sexy, macho man—and he loved her. It was a miracle.

Five minutes later she again studied Timothy and the man he seemed to be talking to. Carly stared intently for a while, then whispered, "Dad?"

"Oh, my goodness, it is Dad!" She kicked her horse in the ribs to get him running and yelled, "Jake, it's Dad! I'm riding ahead!"

Jake felt as though *he'd* just been kicked in the ribs. Talking to Stu on the phone about his and Carly's love affair was one thing; telling Stuart Paxton face-to-face that he was sleeping with his daughter was a whole other ball game.

How did one man admit such a thing to another? Especially when the other guy was his boss?

Fourteen

Carly leaped off her horse before it came to a full stop, dropped the reins and ran at her father—who was striding out to meet her—with her arms open. "Dad, Dad! I can't believe you're here. When did you arrive?"

Laughing, Stuart hugged his daughter. "About an hour ago. Didn't you get the message I left on the answering machine?"

"Uh...when did you leave it?"

"Yesterday."

Carly smiled just a tiny bit sheepishly. "I, uh, haven't been here since yesterday morning. Neither has Jake."

A twinkle entered Stuart's blue eyes. "I see. Well, you look fabulous, Carly. Do you know that you've got stars in your eyes?"

Carly blushed. "We need to talk, Dad. I've got a lot to tell you."

"And I'd say from the roses in your cheeks and the remarkable enthusiasm I see in your eyes that I'm going to like every word.''

''I think so, Dad, yes.''

The men were separating the stallion from the mares, and Carly and Stuart turned to watch. Expertly the cowboys worked the stallion into a small steel holding pen so the vet could examine him. The mares were driven into a corral.

Jake called hello to Timothy, then got off his horse and walked over to Stuart to shake his hand. ''When'd you get here, Stu?''

''About an hour ago. How've you been, Jake?''

''Uh, good, Stu, real good.'' Jake turned to look at the holding pen. ''We finally caught him.''

''He's a beauty, Jake.''

''No argument there, Stu. Timothy, what do you think?'' Jake walked over to the vet, who was conducting his examination from outside of the holding pen.

''The bullet tore his hide open, but it's strictly a flesh wound. Other than that he's in pretty good shape, Jake.''

Stuart had followed and was looking at the stallion with a frown. ''He's been shot?''

''Yeah, that furrow on his rump is a bullet wound,'' Timothy confirmed. ''I'll dose him with antibiotics, clean up the wound and he'll be fine, Stuart.''

''Who shot him, Jake?'' Stuart asked.

''I don't know, Stu. Wish I did, but none of the men will own up to it. I'm going to go and take a look at the mares. Would you like to come with me?''

''Carly wants to talk to me, Jake. I'll see you later.''

''Okay, sure.'' With his heart in his throat and a sinking sensation in his gut, Jake watched Carly and Stuart walk toward the house arm-in-arm.

Today could be his last on Wild Horse Ranch. How could Carly be so smart about other things and so dense about that possibility?

In the house Carly opened the refrigerator and took out a

soda. "What would you like, Dad? Are you hungry? I could make some sandwiches."

"No soda, no sandwiches. I'm fine just the way I am and I'm awfully glad to see you so happy. What happened?"

Carly opened her soda for a swallow. "I fell in love with Jake, Dad," she said simply. "I...think I've changed more than you, or even I, could have imagined before I came here."

"Changed in what way, honey?" Stuart asked gently.

"For one thing I know that I have never been in love before, not like I am now. What I feel for Jake is so big, so overwhelming, so right, Dad, that...that..." Carly stopped and frowned. "I can't explain it."

"You've explained it well enough, Carly. I'm thrilled and happy for you, but you haven't said anything about how Jake feels. Does he love you?"

"Oh, yes! Dad, there's something else. I'm going to stay here. I've come to love the ranch and Wyoming and even this run-down old house, which, of course, I intend to re-model and modernize. Most of it, anyhow. Some of it is charming and just needs a good cleaning or a coat of paint."

Stuart nodded. "So, you and Jake are...what? Going to get married? Live together?"

"Uh, I think we're just going to live together. We...haven't made any definite plans about anything. But we love each other very much." *We're both scared spitless of marriage, Dad. You know my reasons, but Jake is going to have to tell you his. I can't betray his confidence.*

"Carly, this is a delicate question, considering what happened to your first pregnancy, but have you and Jake talked about children? Does he want kids? Do you?"

"No, we haven't discussed...that."

"Well, whatever makes you happy makes me happy, honey." Stuart kissed his daughter's cheek.

"Thank you, Dad. I'm going to run now and take a

shower. You'll probably be out with Jake and the horses when I'm finished, so I'll come outside then.''

''Fine, sweetheart. See you later.''

While showering, Carly went over the conversation with her dad. He was happy for her, but she knew him well enough to read between the lines: he would rather have her and Jake married than living together without marriage.

The thing was, so would she prefer marriage. But Jake wouldn't and didn't, and if she loved him—which she did— she had to take him as he was, dark moods and all. She wished now that she hadn't said such awful things about love and marriage last night, because while all that malice was true about her first experience with serious romance, it wasn't even remotely true with Jake. It was odd how clearly she knew that, because what real proof did she have? But know it she did, and how did a woman explain such a monumental change of attitude to the man she loved?

And a final straw, it seemed to Carly, was that she had sworn an oath to never disappoint or worry her father again, and she had broken her vow. He would never come right out and say it to her face, but he didn't have to; she knew he was terribly disappointed with her decision to live with Jake without the benefit of marriage.

Silent tears rolled down her cheeks and mixed with the shower water.

Jake had pulled Timothy away from the stallion so the vet could take a look at the mares. Stuart walked up to the corral they were in. ''Jake, come take a little walk with me.''

''Sure thing, Stu.'' Jake figured this was it. Carly had told her dad about the two of them, and Stuart was not going to permit it to go on. Climbing between two of the corral's rails, Jake joined his boss. ''Sorry I wasn't here when you arrived,'' he said as the two men began walking away from the corrals and barns.

''No problem. Don't worry about it. Jake, Carly just told

me that the two of you are going to be living together. She said she loves both you and the ranch and is going to stay in Wyoming.''

Stuart Paxton had always been a soft-spoken man around Jake, and his voice was no more strident today than usual. But Jake heard something in it he'd not heard before, and he tried to put meaning to the discordant note. Stuart didn't sound angry, annoyed or indignant, he decided. Was it uneasy? Troubled? Apprehensive?

Regardless, Stu had laid his cards on the table, and Jake knew that he had to do the same. If ever he'd needed to step up to the plate and prove that he was a man of principle, it was now.

"I love her, Stu," he said quietly, belying the thunderous pounding of his heart. And before Stuart could respond to that declaration, Jake added, "I'd like your permission to ask Carly to marry me."

Stuart never said a word, just kept plodding along next to Jake with his hands in his pockets. Jake, feeling a little sick to his stomach, figured that Stuart was thinking of all the reasons why his daughter should not be involved with a cowboy, and probably trying to come up with a way to say it without totally destroying Jake's ego. For a few moments Jake actually had to squelch a silly, adolescent urge to recite his good points.

Finally Stuart asked, "Does Carly know you're considering marriage?"

A bolt of lightning could not have jarred Jake more. Wasn't Stuart going to object to the relationship at all?

"Truth is," Jake said, sounding a little hoarse because of his dry mouth, "I wasn't...until now."

"And the idea just sort of came flying out of nowhere?"

"Uh, not really. I did think of it before this, but I never dared to hope... I mean..." Jake forced himself to calm down. "Stu, she's your daughter."

"My only daughter, Jake. My only child," Stuart murmured.

"I know."

"Don't sound so miserable. Anyone who loves their children wants only happiness for them, Jake, and if you continue to make Carly as happy as she is today, that's far more than I can do." Stuart stopped walking and laid his hand on Jake's shoulder. "Ask her, Jake, but don't be surprised if she says no. I think that when it comes to marriage, Carly's a little gun-shy."

"She told me about her marriage."

"And the miscarriage?"

"Yes."

"That's a hell of a good start to a long-term relationship, Jake. She's in the house, cleaning up. Why don't you go talk to her now, and maybe we'll have reason to celebrate tonight."

Jake stuck out his hand. "Thanks, Stu."

"For what? I only want what's best for Carly, Jake."

Jake grinned. "Yeah, but I never expected the best to be me."

Carly had rushed through a shower and shampoo. She was dressed in clean jeans and shirt, and she was brushing her hair in front of the bureau mirror in her bedroom when she heard someone bounding up the stairs. Stepping into the hall, she smiled in pleased surprise when she saw Jake.

"Shower time for you, too?" she asked.

"Something a lot more important than that, sweetheart." Taking her arm, Jake steered her back into her bedroom. "Your dad and I just had a talk."

"So did we. Dad and I, I mean. We talked before I showered, and I told him about us."

"Yes, he said you told him that we're going to live together."

"We are, aren't we?" Carly suddenly felt uneasy, and suspicious of something she was afraid of defining.

"Your dad is one great guy," Jake said.

"Yes, he is. Jake, why are you wearing that silly grin? What's going on?"

"I have your father's permission to ask you to marry me," Jake said proudly.

Carly stared. "You...don't mean it."

"Did I say something wrong?"

Carly stumbled over to a chair and fell into it. "Jake, I know how you feel about marriage. Did...did Dad put you up to this?"

"Carly, what're you talking about? Stu and I had a talk. That's all that happened."

Carly studied him through a frown of serious concentration. Finally she said, "I don't think so. And before you disagree, think back on your conversation with Dad and tell me if you picked up any strange vibes from him. Anything at all out of the ordinary."

Jake frowned, too. "Well, yes, there was something, but I still don't know what it was."

"It was the same thing I felt when he and I were talking, Jake. He doesn't like the idea of our just living together."

"Did you, uh, tell him that we've *been* living together?" Jake asked, sounding nervous about it.

"We haven't been living together, we've slept together a few times. Jake, are you afraid of Dad?"

Jake looked at her long and hard. "I don't blame you for asking that question, Carly, because that's the way I've been behaving. No, I'm not afraid of your dad, but I do respect him as a man and what he's made of his life, and I never believed that he would sanction a relationship between you, his only child, and one of his hired hands. When I realized I was falling for you, I fought against it because of my past and because of my job."

"Oh, Jake," Carly said sadly. "And now you think you have to marry me."

Jake rushed over to her and knelt at her knees. "I don't have to do anything. Neither do you. Carly, we've both put in some hard time. Don't we deserve better?" He took her hands. "Sweetheart, I never dared to let myself admit it, but I'm admitting it now. I want it all, marriage, a family, a real home. I want you, Carly. I love you and I want you for my wife. Will you marry me?"

Tears filled Carly's eyes. "I would be happy just living with you, Jake."

"And if that's what you want, I'd be happy just living with you, Carly." Jake's eyes were suspiciously moist and expectant. Very expectant.

"You...you're quite serious about this," she said, sounding choked up.

"Carly, I believed with every cell in my body that I would never say those words again, but I'm saying them to you. Would you honor me by becoming my wife?"

She lovingly laid her hands on his face and looked into his hopeful blue eyes. "Jake, would we live happily ever after?"

"Yes, my love, we would live happily ever after. I promise." Jake gathered her into his arms and held her close to his heart. "I love you. You are the love of my life."

"You are the love of *my* life, darling Jake," she whispered huskily, trying hard not to just let go and sob. "Yes, I'll marry you."

They left the house a short time later, holding hands. Stuart saw them coming and knew at once what had occurred. He met them halfway.

No one played coy or minced words. "We're getting married," Carly and Jake said, almost in unison.

Stuart smiled, kissed his daughter and shook Jake's hand. "I couldn't be more pleased."

"Hey, Jake," Timothy yelled from the steel holding pen. "You'd better take a look at this."

All three of them hurried over to the pen. "What is it?" Jake asked.

"I thought you said this big stallion was wild."

"He is." Jake frowned. "Isn't he?"

Timothy worked the stallion's mouth open. "I wanted to know his age, and, as you know, Jake, teeth are the best way to make that estimate. But look at what I found."

Jake took a look. "Well, I'll be damned."

"What?" Carly asked anxiously. "What is it?"

"A lip tattoo," Jake told her and explained further as Stuart moved over to the pen to have a look himself. "This stallion didn't come into this world as a wild horse. He belongs to someone, or he used to. That tattoo can be checked with various horse-breeding and registration associations. We'll be able to track down his owner now and return him to his rightful home."

"Oh, no," Carly cried. "Oh, Jake, I wanted him to be mine from the moment I saw him." Then she realized how that sounded and she shaped a smile for the love of her life. "On the other hand, I think it was you that I wanted at first sight."

Jake threw back his head and laughed. "Ditto, sweetheart."

And from the side of the holding pen, where he was still standing, Stuart Paxton heaved a completely contented sigh.

He had successfully instigated and completed dozens of important, money-making projects and deals in his career, but not one of them came close to giving him the satisfaction that he felt now over having dreamed up the perfect solution to both Carly's and Jake's personal miseries.

Yes, indeed, talking Carly into coming to the ranch for a summer visit had been a brilliant idea.

Absolutely brilliant.

* * * * *

COMING NEXT MONTH

#1303 BACHELOR DOCTOR—Barbara Boswell
Man of the Month
He was brilliant, handsome—and couldn't keep his mind off nurse
Callie Sheely! No one had ever captured Dr. Trey Weldon's attention
like Callie, but she insisted their relationship would never work. Could
Trey convince Callie otherwise with a soul-stirring seduction…?

#1304 MIDNIGHT FANTASY—Ann Major
Body & Soul
Tag rescued Claire when she was in dire peril—and then showed her
the delights of true fantasy. Could this very real man of her dreams
save Claire from even greater danger—marriage to the wrong man?

#1305 WIFE FOR HIRE—Amy J. Fetzer
Wife, Inc.
What horse breeder Nash Rayburn needed was a temporary wife. What
he got was Hayley Albright, his former lover and soon-to-be doctor.
But Hayley still carried a torch for Nash. Could she rekindle *his* love—
this time permanently?

#1306 RIDE A WILD HEART—Peggy Moreland
Texas Grooms
Bronc rider Pete Dugan always knew that he was not cut out to be a
family man—then Carol Benson walked back into his life. Carol had
commitment written all over her, but when she revealed her long-held
secret, would Pete be ready to say "I do"?

#1307 BLOOD BROTHERS—Anne McAllister and Lucy Gordon
2-in-1 Original Stories
Double trouble! That's what you got when cousins Montana cowboy
Gabe McBride and British lord Randall Stanton traded places. What
Gabe and Randall got was the challenge of their lives—wooing the
women of their hearts. Because to win Claire McBride and Frederika
Crossman, these two blood brothers would need to exert all their
British pluck and cowboy try!

#1308 COWBOY FOR KEEPS—Kristi Gold
Single mom Dana Landry cared only about catering to the special
needs of her daughter. Then cowboy Will Baker taught Dana she had
to take care of *her* needs, as well—and he was just the man to help.
But when the night was over, would Will still want to be Dana's
cowboy for keeps?

CMN0600